MIDNIGHT CARTEL 2

Chris Green

Lock Down Publications and
Ca$h
Presents
Midnight Cartel 2
A Novel by *Chris Green*

Chris Green

Lock Down Publications
P.O. Box 870494
Mesquite, Tx 75187

Visit our website @
www.lockdownpublications.com

Copyright 2020 by Chris Green
Midnight Cartel 2

First Edition March 2020
Printed in the United States of America

Lock Down Publications
Like our page on Facebook: Lock Down Publications @
www.facebook.com/lockdownpublications.ldp
Cover design and layout by: **Dynasty Cover Me**
Book interior design by: **Shawn Walker**
Edited by: **Jill Duska**

Stay Connected with Us!

Text **LOCKDOWN** to 22828 to stay up-to-date with new releases, sneak peaks, contests and more…

Thank you.

Submission Guideline.

Submit the first three chapters of your completed manuscript to ldpsubmissions@gmail.com, subject line: Your book's title. The manuscript must be in a .doc file and sent as an attachment. Document should be in Times New Roman, double spaced and in size 12 font. Also, provide your synopsis and full contact information. If sending multiple submissions, they must each be in a separate email.

Have a story but no way to send it electronically? You can still submit to LDP/Ca$h Presents. Send in the first three chapters, written or typed, of your completed manuscript to:

LDP: Submissions Dept
Po Box 870494
Mesquite, Tx 75187

DO NOT send original manuscript. Must be a duplicate.

Provide your synopsis and a cover letter containing your full contact information.

Thanks for considering LDP and Ca$h Presents.

Acknowledgments

The last time I was writing these, I nearly shouted out to everybody I could. So this is the next book that I've been trying to construct for my readers. *Midnight Cartel* is a key to my legacy and holds a significance to one of my favorite novels written by me. Of course, the last book for this series will wrap up to show a mystery that you guys will not be expecting.

This book game has been a very fun experience, and I'm extremely excited about getting closer to walking out of this gate to pursue those dreams further. I love you all, from my daughter to my mother to my brothers to my crew - I mean my real crew. Thank you. Of course, my readers and fans, the people who never seem to deny my pen, I love you all so much.

Peace. LDP love and never quit at anything you would like to succeed. Remember, you're unique.

Chris Green

Chapter 1

Ryan couldn't help but glance at everyone who surrounded the table. No one looked happy to be there, and when Richard spoke, everyone gave him their full attention. Two redheaded women posted behind him. Guns were attached to each of their hips, and the weird expressions on their faces stated that debating wasn't in the conference schedule.

"Now last week, I clarified a matter to the ones who needed to know. I've been the same since you all first began, and I will be the same when you leave. "

Still, no one said anything. The murderous thoughts of a set up crossed Ryan's mind when Richard rose to his feet. Richard walked over to his small blue bar and fixed himself a small glass of red wine. He took a sip and inhaled deeply before speaking

"Winter, Summer, please take care of the business."

Ryan watched the two women step off the wall. They each removed a pistol and gunned down the man sitting directly next to Ryan.

The blood splatter from the man's brains sprinkled softly on Ryan's shirt. The man's heavy corpse fell roughly towards the floor as the women found their places back on the wall.

Ryan wiped the side of his face and kept his composure. The quick movement had his stomach on the floor, and he surely didn't want to be next. Before he could reach for his gun, Richard began to talk.

"I don't tolerate snitches, people. It's already problems with the cops who are sliding around here now, and we don't need any more. Who brought that guy here?"

Everyone cut their eyes slowly over to Detective Cross. His face was pale, and his eyes read the words "GUILTY" in bold letters.

"Cross, the north side has been disgraced by your client. He has failed to meet our requirements, and that falls back on you. What do you have to say for yourself?" Richard removed the top piece of his suit.

He couldn't muster a word. Fear consumed him, but he refused to die in vain. "I was about to get rid of him, sir. I warned him about the problems and heat. I never knew that he was already giving information to the Feds."

"You know when we deal with police, it's on a short leash. Is that correct, Detective Cross?

His head nodded in a quick motion, and his collar was beginning to soak up the sweat that was running down from his temple.

"Then you know that we don't tolerate mistakes. Do you feel that just because you're a cop, we won't handle you accordingly? I'm in charge for a reason, and the boss lady ain't too happy right now. Where does that leave us, Cross?" Richard folded his arms impatiently.

"I don't know, sir."

Laughing loudly, Richard clapped his hands. The table members continued to sit in silence. "This guy doesn't even know. That's just grand. A criminal cop that doesn't know the reason for us losing money. It's the same reason you don't know why you're dying by the hands of your own." His face tightened with anger.

Stepping from the back room, Bradley grabbed everyone's attention. He removed his holstered pistol. He aimed for Cross's head and pulled the trigger.

Boom!

Richard stood in place with a straight face. His eyes roamed back and forth over the twelve members of his organization. No one moved an inch. The room was silent. The blue light that dangled above them flickered, causing him to smile. "That concludes the problems. We've suffered at the hands of these fools but now, business can continue. "

Bradley made his way smoothly back through the door. Before closing it, he locked eyes with Ryan and winked.

Taking a seat at the table, Richard glanced at his watch. "So, to clear things up a bit. Ryan will be the new runner of the north side. You were brought here for a reason, and I pray it wasn't to waste my time. We have a seven hour time span until everyone in the regular world starts to move. You can handle this, right?" Richard was glaring into his eyes.

"Without a question," Ryan replied.

After slapping both of his hands together, Richard sparked his cigar. "We got us an arrogant man here. I like arrogant. It shows me that you're ready to sacrifice anything. I mean anything. Even if it costs your life," he whispered in a low tone.

Ryan continued to hold eye contact. There was only one way he knew to go out. The mystery of the man in front of him still placed his mind in a puzzling maze. Being the king of the north side sounded great, so the details could come later.

"Let me clarify something to you all. My job is to make sure you move as delicately as possible. We operate for the team. Not for self. Money is to be made, and slackers will not be tolerated. Summer and Winter's job is to place a bullet through your skull if you can't complete that." Richard pointed to the redheaded women behind him.

The members still collectively remained quiet.

"Great. That concludes another meeting, guys. Before we leave, I want to introduce you all to Ryan. Embrace him. We're all family here. Maybe on the next check in, you can be greeted the proper way. Sorry about the clothes. I'll be sure to throw you in some spending money for a new wardrobe." Richard poured himself another drink.

"I'm not trying to sit back and wait for another fall, Richard. This is our third city, and I'm not into moving anymore," Simion from Atlanta spoke up.

Not only was he the number one honcho for Atlanta's drug supply, his lucrative businesses gave him the capability to play with numbers like a twenty year professional. He was in charge of the south border, and his money blessed the cartel with a healthy baseline. His tall, dark-skinned frame could tower easily over anyone under the height of 5'10". He kept a low haircut, and his hands always rested over his knee like he was a 1950s pimp. Still and all, Simion was known to rule with an iron fist. It was the reason he was so wealthy at such a young age.

"Simion, this is not about to be a repeat. I can guarantee that. Everyone, maintain your stations and push things back together. I have a feeling about the new kid. He looks trustworthy." Richard puffed on his cigar with a sinister smile.

The meeting paused when Lizzy pranced around the corner with excitement. Moving over to Richard, she leaned down and whispered something into his ear.

Richard rose to his feet. He checked his watch. "This meeting is officially coming to a close. I think we all know what the next mission is, so please be careful. New kid, pick your bag up from Lizzy. I don't know what you're used to moving, but forty is the limit. No more than two weeks. We don't speak on these meetings unless you're ready for your death date. Understood?" Richard asked Ryan with a raised eyebrow.

"Yeah, I got it."

"Good."

"I'll see all of you in two weeks. Meeting adjourned." Richard smiled before heading into the back office with Summer and Winter behind him.

Ryan got up from his seat. Everyone exited the room and headed back upstairs for the bar.

The atmosphere of everything seemed to go back to normal when he crossed the door into the bar's floor. Members of the cartel moved to different sections and occupied their private spaces. Drinks began to flow, and before Ryan could take a few steps over to the counter, Lizzy set a black garbage bag on the bar top.

"Hun, the deal was for you to take the trash out. I don't have time to debate," she said with a joking smile.

Ryan looked around at all the customers vibing to the music. He grabbed the bag and proceeded to the door.

The entire moment felt so unreal. He came to this meeting unaware of who was in charge. Ryan witnessed shit that was supposed to be close and personal. It was evident that he was dealing with some people who were truly as about the business as they portrayed themselves to be. Now he was walking out of the building with forty keys of cocaine on his back. The thought of a bullet ripping through the back of his head forced him to speed it up a notch.

Stepping outside, he moved past the two guards and headed for his Infiniti truck. After tossing the heavy sack in the back, he climbed into the driver's seat and calmly pulled away.

His eyes couldn't help but to glance back and forth into his rearview mirror. The thought of calling Bradley scurried through his mind, but he decided quickly that it may not be a good idea. The night of his introduction, he watched a crooked cop murder his own partner in cold blood. Bradley was beyond crooked. He was a criminal by heart, one who couldn't be trusted. Even still, he was the one that introduced Ryan to the main plug, Richard. No one was able to meet the man and walk away with forty bricks on the first sit down. It was unheard of. The cartel was unnoticed, a midnight crew that migrated together for the cause of making money. Not just that, but they kept it within a circle where none besides them could have the chance of eating off the plate. It was called organized crime.

Sliding across the bridge in his luxury vehicle, Ryan dialed DJ's number, heading for the Northside of Philly.

* * *

DJ, Ryan's house, Philadelphia, 2:23 a. m.

Knocking on Ryan's door with anger, DJ looked up and down through his window until the locks detached. Ryan peeped his head out.

"What's good, man? You a'ight?" DJ stepped inside his crib after he cracked the door.

"Lower your voice. The neighbors can hear you through the walls." Ryan locked the door behind them and waved him to living room.

The sight of all the keys tensed up DJ's body instantly. It was usual to see a brick or maybe two. Coming up in the game was hard. It took grinding and tough work to get a real business off the ground.

DJ walked over to the table. He snapped his head back to Ryan. "Where the fuck did you get this from, bro?

"I met someone. They decided to help me out. This is what we got."

"You met someone that gave you forty kilos of cocaine? Ryan, what the fuck did you do?"

"I didn't do shit, nigga. That's on Kimyetta. I just told you. I met somebody. I can't explain it because I'm not allowed to speak on this business. All you need to know is that we straight. I found the way, and I need your help." He stared at DJ with a serious face.

DJ glanced back down at all the work. He picked one up. "What do we gotta do, man?

15

Smiling, Ryan grabbed a pen and piece of paper from the kitchen drawer. He sat at the table and scribbled down a few items they would need. "This is the way I see it. These people want $18,000 for every brick. If we off all of them, we will have $280,000 to split after we pay them the rest. We ain't never touched no paper like that."

Nodding slowly, DJ contemplated the thought. "I'm down with it, but how many people do we got to have beside us to make sure we win? There's no way in hell we can get off forty of these things by our damn self. "

Ryan stood up. "We can just build our own little team. Just the loyal ones. All we trying to do is get this money to make more money. The quicker we get it off, the less problems on our hands. We have Sekoya. "

"Sekoya isn't enough, Ryan. We need shooters. This ain't no ounce of weed we talking about." DJ stood against the wall, waiting for a reply.

"We might need to do some recruiting. I'm not just sliding no anybody on our side, bro. It's hard enough dealing with Bradley. Delaware is our stomping ground. I'm not trying to burn this spot down here in Philly until I buy me a house with straight cash. For right now, it's me and you. And we got two weeks."

Rubbing the hair on his chin, DJ clicked on his grind mode. "If we gon' do it, we gotta knock all competitors out the way. Even if it costs us to get shorted on the end."

"Fuck that. As long as we eating and have this money added up correctly for these people, I wouldn't care. We can build this shit from the ground until we got enough money to say fuck it. "

Shrugging his shoulders, DJ picked up one brick. "Let's get to work."

Chris Green

Chapter 2

Faith's home, 8:35 a.m.

Faith dialed Ryan's number for the tenth time. She hung up the line and picked Prince up from his car seat. His curly hair and beady little eyes were an exact replica of Ryan. Faith was in a hard position. Having the father of her child run the streets was easier when there wasn't a baby in the picture. Now that he was finally here, Ryan had taken more of a dip into the terror of Delaware. Graduation was approaching, and shit was surely about to become more critical if he happened to take a loss with the police or prison system.

Watching her mother enter the front door, Faith cleared her mind with the negative thinking.

"Are you alright?" She looked into Faith's eyes.

Not trying to bring up the conversation, she nodded. "I'll be fine, Mama."

"Says who? From this spot I'm standing in, it looks like you're not. Has that boy been stressing you out again?" Ms. Anderson questioned with anger.

As she rocked little Prince in her arms, a few tears began to form around her pupils. "Am I gonna be doing this by myself, Mama? Is it really gonna be like this for my baby?"

Exhaling, she shook her head before wiping Faith's cheek. "This is the reality of the real world, baby girl. I warned you to be careful on how you moved with this overgrown-ass kid. He's still a child himself, so it would be impossible. What's making you waste your time like this, Faith? Ryan is so obnoxious and filled with his own desires. It's the path of most thugs like himself. You gotta step up. Put his ass up for child support. The stupid shit that he does in the streets could easily spill back on you and Prince. Don't sit back and wait until it's too late." Ms. Anderson stood up and left Faith to herself.

There was pain in Faith's heart for the family she desired so badly. Ryan was in the position to make decisions instead of taking the orders. That alone empowered his mind to believe that the King of Delaware truly held a purpose. He was lost in a world of his own, and Faith wasn't about to stick around and wait for the results. If he didn't change his thinking process, she was taking the issue to a new level before her family experienced any backlash from Ryan's irrational thinking. She was going to sit him down for a serious intervention - one that came with no options.

* * *

DJ, Ryan's house

Feeling his phone vibrate for what felt like the hundredth time, DJ rolled over from Ryan's couch and answered.

"Hello?"

"DJ, where the hell are you? I've been blowing your phone up. Have you heard about what's going on?" Rose said impatiently.

"No, I was down at Ryan's new spot and ended up falling asleep. What's wrong?" He yawned while wiping the corner of his eyes.

"Wicked got shot and he at Dupoint. Reckless tried to rob the wrong people. Bae, they saying he might not make it."

"What!" DJ jumped up from under the covers. "Who the hell you hear this from?"

"The entire hood know. They tried someone out on the east side - "

"Stop. Don't say anything else on the phone." He stopped her before she could go into detail. "Meet us at the hospital in thirty minutes."

After hanging up the line, DJ wasted no time storming into Ryan's room and nudging him. He began to stir from his sleep.

"What's good, bro? You 'bout to leave?"

"No. Wicked got shot. We gotta get down to the hospital. "

"What?"

"Yeah, Rose told me he's down at Dupoint. We need to go."

Scrambling to his feet, Ryan rushed to clean himself up. After throwing on a Calvin Klein sweat suit, he placed on a pair of wheat Timberland boots. It was hard for him to hear something about one of his own getting hurt. Out of his entire crew, he had gained a great bond with Wicked that remained unbroken. Even after the recent beef with Reckless, Ryan continued to encourage Wicked to operate with the winning team. His mission was to make sure that all of them ate. When there happened to be a nigga around who was on the leader position shit, things tended to go extremely sour. Robbing wasn't on the list anymore, but you could never take the ghetto out of a hoodlum either. It was the reason Ryan decided to let them tread down their own path.

After throwing on their coats, they headed out of the spot en route to Delaware.

* * *

Reckless, Dupoint Hospital

Shuffling around in the hospital's patient area, Reckless watched as the doctors moved in and out of Wicked's room. He had set up a recent robbery last week. He did his research and the move was guaranteed to set them both straight for the rest of their lives. It was their way out. Unfortunately, they received inaccurate information, which led to his cousin being in critical condition. The bullet had pierced his chest four inches away from the heart. The sound of the gun continued to ring in his mind as he paced back and forth.

He had no explanation for his mother and aunt. Flying from Arizona to Delaware for his funeral was something he didn't have the courage to tell their relatives.

His thoughts crashed when he spotted DJ and Ryan step inside of the waiting area. Instantly, he rose to his feet, clutching the side of his hip.

"What the fuck happened?" DJ glared at him with fire dancing in his pupils.

"Who the fuck is you, nigga, the cops? You see that he got fucking shot." Reckless's reply was short and direct.

"He asked you how the fuck did it happen, nigga!" Ryan said with more authority. His eyes were slanted and the anger was ready to release minutes before he even arrived at the hospital.

Before he could respond with his slick remark, Ryan closed the small gap in between them. His pistol slid from the waist with expertise. "Buck, nigga. On

Kim, I'll spill yo' shit in the hospital. Kill all that making a scene shit, because if you wanted to see me, for real, we could've handled it in the street. Wicked is my fucking friend. That's the reason I'm here. If you got a problem with that, bust a move!" Ryan clenched his jaw.

Reckless's hands began to move in a fidgety motion. The waiting room was empty, and he did not have back up on his side. The thought of Wicked seeing their situation at hand forced him to build up his manhood. His gangster was pushing on the turf, and it wasn't gonna stop just because Ryan was laying down his dirt nap game.

Stepping in between them, DJ placed a hand on each of their chests. By this time, Reckless was removing his gun from his waistline.

"You got me fucked up, pussy. Just because you feel that you burning shit doesn't mean I won't pop back. You claim you here for my cousin. I don't see why. It's obvious that we on opposite teams, nigga. Real potnas get money together. You don't shine on us because you feel that y'all winning," he spat, cutting his eyes over to DJ.

"Nigga, we ain't yo' bitch. I told y'all fools that we ain't robbing no more. I offered yo' duck ass a way out, to get some money where we can be straight. I got a son already, pussy boy. Stop trying to give me a second one."

Before DJ could get them to end the fruitless conversation, a detective dressed in a beige suit stepped out of Wicked's room. His eyes landed directly on the guns before Ryan and Reckless could try to conceal them.

"Is there a problem here?" he questioned, exposing his holstered weapon. His bushy eyebrows were connected like a straight line. He stood at an even six feet, and his light tan would give you the impression that he wanted to be black.

"No, sir. Were just waiting to see my brother." DJ stepped in front of them both.

"Sure you are. I'm not worried about the weapons because the first one to shoot a gun in this hospital around these innocent people will be dead before you can record your name to the medical staff. My name is Detective Furlow, better known as Mr. Lock 'Em the Fuck Up!" he yelled with a crooked smile. "I don't mean to be a hard ass, but your friend who was shot is now a suspect to a robbery. He's going to jail. Now the only thing about is this: he wasn't the only criminal to commit this vicious act. I mean, if I was the one getting robbed, I would've probably stood over the cocksucker and blown his brains out, but that's just me. My point is, if you're not involved with this guy, then you guys might wanna get the hell out of here before I place all of you under arrest until I can find out who's my second man on this case. "

Upon hearing his statement, Reckless walked smoothly off towards the opposite direction.

"Sir, I don't mean any disrespect. The only reason we're down here is because our friend was hurt. We don't know anything about any robbery or what not. I understand that you have a job to do, but we have a right to make sure he's okay. He's like our family," DJ spoke with sincerity.

"You actually might be the first black guy that I've liked since high school, son." Furlow smirked. "Unfortunately, that doesn't mean a damn thing to me. I have a job to do, and that's searching for whatever culprit tried to rob these innocent people. "

Stepping in front of DJ, Ryan grabbed the bridge of his nose. "Excuse me. I'm not sure if you're a fucking cop or a KKK clan member, but we don't give a fuck. The same way you have a job, we have a family. It's about respect. We haven't come at you sideways, so I would like to ask you to please calm down," Ryan said sternly.

Looking him up and down, Detective Furlow chuckled. "That was very funny, young man. You should've been on that funny TV show with that weird guy Martin. See, what I can do for you is throw your ass in custody for that illegal weapon on your hip. Then I can call a couple of my KKK members, as you put it, to drag your ass straight down to the institution. I would watch my tongue if I were you."

"No one is trying to be on your shit list, but have a little compassion. All we want to do is check on our friend to make sure he's okay. After that, sir, we will leave." Ryan wouldn't let up.

Wiggling a finger, Furlow smiled. "That sure sounds a lot better. I'll tell you what we can do. I'll let you go in alone and speak to him for three minutes. I'm going to stand right here by this door with your friend right here. If it takes you any longer than the given time to exit, you'll be leaving in handcuffs. "

"I don't need nothing but one."

Furlow stepped to the side and allowed Ryan to enter Wicked's room. The sight of him lying in the bed alone sent chills down his spine, not to mention all the funny ass machines that sat around beeping and shit. It gave him thoughts about the way his dad was handled in prison. No one wanted to feel death closing in. It was the reason Ryan handled business accordingly. No man would ever be able to get a glimpse of him slipping. Luckily, Wicked had been spared by the grace of God.

Wicked looked up into Ryan's eyes. "What's good, brother?" Wicked spoke in a raspy tone.

"What's up, bro? How you feeling?"

"I'm a'ight. This shit hurt, but I only got hit in the shoulder and stomach. This medicine got my head floating."

"What the fuck made you go out there like that, Wicked? I told you to come eat with me. You're sitting in a bed with a pair of handcuffs connecting you to the bed. You're about to get put in jail for some miscellaneous shit, and Reckless don't give a damn."

The expression on Wicked's face explained everything that needed to be said. The only thing he could do was drop a small tear. "He's my cousin, Ryan. I don't have no choice but to stand by him. "

"Nigga, you got a choice to stand by yourself. Reckless is gonna get you fucking killed, bro. This detective is standing outside of your door waiting to send yo' ass up dirt creek. I'm gonna let you know this. I'll look into making sure you good until we can talk without these extra ears. Besides that, I love you, bro. This fake-ass beef with Reckless is gonna pull you away from me if he ain't changing his movements up. Me and DJ are about to win. After all this shit is over between you and this little case, I'm gonna make sure you good. "

"I just want you to do one thing for me, Ryan," Wicked stressed. He was breathing erratically.

"What?

"Just graduate."

Shaking his head with slight doubt, Ryan looked into Wicked's eyes. "If it's meant to happen, I'll walk across that stage. Hopefully you'll be able to make bail or something where I can see you step across with everybody else. I know this may be hard to understand, but Reckless is too much for me, and the only way you're gonna be able to rock on my side is if you get his ass to calm down before he pulls some shit that he can't take back. "

"I'll talk to him, bro." Wicked's eyes cast down to the floor.

Just from the expression, Ryan could tell that the statement floated completely through the other side of his head. It was the same reason that Ryan wouldn't hesitate to bury Reckless if he slipped and pulled the wrong stunt. The only thing he could do was give it time to see. The new business at hand was a golden opportunity, and nothing would defeat his new mission of reigning high. Delaware would soon be his play home.

"I have to go. You have a pig right outside of your door, and I'm not trying to become familiar with this motherfucker." Ryan tapped Wicked's leg and headed for the door.

"Don't hurt him, Ryan. I know he's hard to deal with, but he's still my cousin."

Without turning around, Ryan nodded and left the room.

As Ryan stepped back into the lobby, he looked at Detective Furlow, who stood in his same position with an arrogant smirk. "I see you have great timing, Mr. Delaware. Hopefully I'll see you around. "

"What the fuck did you just call me?" Ryan's adrenaline began to slightly rush from the remark.

Grabbing him by his shoulder, DJ quickly pulled him towards the hospital exit. "Don't let him trick you, Ryan. He's a cop."

"I wouldn't give a fuck. Did you just hear what that nigga said?"

"Yeah, I did, and regardless of how weird it may sounded, you have to understand that your name is hotter than a fucking jalapeño pepper. You know his many times I've heard that shit in the past three weeks? It means you need to calm down and start calculating yo' steps better," DJ warned him.

Fixing the sleeve of his shirt, Ryan hocked a glob of spit on the ground. "I wouldn't give a fuck what anybody has heard. If the police screaming shit like that, it makes me think a nigga speaking instead of letting these bitches listen. It's one mistake in his crooked-ass statement. My dad was Mr. Delaware. I'm gonna be the king of this bitch. It's a difference."

"And I stand behind all that, but it's still a way we need to move. Don't you think this would be the perfect time to start recruiting? It damn sure isn't possible without the right niggas by our side. That's a lot of shit, Ryan."

After climbing inside the whip, Ryan buckled his seatbelt and looked over to DJ. "I agree, but as I told you from the jump, you're not supposed to even know about this shit. I'm not even sure who the fuck I want to drop the weight off on. I can't slip, period."

"Nigga, you acting like these folks work for Don Corleone. How bad can it be?" DJ lightly nudged his shoulder with a smile.

Ryan couldn't help but to look at him with a blank face. His expression alone said enough.

"Well damn, are you sure it's safe to even trap this shit out?"

"Yeah, I'm sure, I just need to do it discreetly without causing too many people to be alert. Niggas in Wilmington ain't toting like this. These people are powerful, bro. Big enough to feed our entire family to the fucking sharks. Like I said, I need to move quietly, and that means we need some niggas who is smoother than baby oil to come help us bunk this shit. We got two weeks."

Sitting back in his seat, DJ pondered before he spoke. "You always got Torey."

Smacking his teeth, Ryan pulled out of the parking lot. "My cousin? Man, that nigga don't wanna do nothing but kill niggas for fun. I kill niggas for a purpose. To gain. He on the east side losing his mind for nothing, so what makes you feel that he'll be able to function when it comes down to moving bricks of dope?"

"Family, bro. A nigga can't concentrate on shit when he gotta save his damn self, but on the strength of flesh and blood, people will be willing to tighten up on anything. He's still your damn cousin." DJ shrugged. "Not to mention, niggas know not to play with Torey. That man halfway past throwed, and if you ain't trying to get shot, you'll mind your mouth, and just let him be. He's quiet too."

"Maybe. It depends. Torey is more of a bodyguard type. Not to mention he's on my distant side of the family. I've never really had a chance to bond with this nigga, and I don't need him trying to pull no slick shit on me."

"It's all a part of testing him out. We won't know until we try, Ryan."

Ryan pondered what DJ was saying. He couldn't help but agree. There was a quota to meet with the table of the Midnight Cartel and Richard surely was standing sternly on that two week rule. Getting murdered wasn't on his bucket list any time soon, so making the funds was the only avenue. In order to see if proper, he was gonna need a game plan, one that involved a lot of followers. Blind followers, of course.

* * *

After pulling into the parking lot of his Philly home, Ryan and DJ stepped out and headed up the small flight of steps. He never noticed Faith sitting in the small Honda Accord that was parked in front of his building until she stepped out with Prince in her hands.

"Ryan!"

Ryan jerked his head around to make sure he wasn't hearing shit. He grabbed the bridge of his nose. "Faith? How in the fuck did you find my apartment, and I know you don't have my fucking son out here in this cold-ass weather?" he snarled.

"Why, Ryan? What you got to hide way out here in Philly? I been sitting on the house with Prince, and

I still haven't seen you come through to have one parenting conversation about how we about to raise this boy. We need to talk." She tooted up her lips like she was paying some bills and shit.

"The only thing you gonna be talking to is my fucking fist if you don't get the fuck back across that bridge to Delaware with my son. You haven't even gave me time to handle my own business before you approach me about what I'm going to do with you. That's all you care about, me and you. I told you that he's gonna be good. What more do you want, silly-ass girl?"

"First of all, I want you to watch yo' mouth. DJ, you're just gonna sit there and watch him speak like that to me, but you're supposed to be the good influence? Both of y'all are full of bullshit!"

"Faith, don't aggravate the situation."

"Aggravate the situation? Nigga, this is his baby!"

Before Ryan could ease back down the steps, he spotted Precious's 2016 Lexus coupe coming to a halt in front of his two story home. Following his eyes to the vehicle, Faith watched as she stepped out of the car with a handful of fast food.

"Hey Ryan, I brought lunch with me." She smiled brightly from ear to ear.

She noticed the silence and looks on all their blank faces. She held the bags in her hand. The tension was uneasy. She realized the female was mugging her up and down. Precious shuffled the bags to one side and extended her hand. "Hi, you must be Faith. I've heard a lot about you."

Jerking back from her hand as if it was an airborne disease, Faith looked at Ryan. "Is this why you can't spend time with your child? Because you playing house with this bitch?"

"Faith, watch your fucking mouth."

"No, fuck that. You need to tell me what it is so I can know how to handle this shit from here on out. My mama told me you wasn't shit. I'm standing right here with your child and you're treating me like I'm a side piece. I need to know where we stand."

"We don't stand on shit! What's hard to understand about that? I told you that I would take care of my child, and you consistently play this dumb role like I owe you something. "

"Ryan, I'm just gonna go and come back at another time." Precious turned around to leave.

"Nah, you ain't going nowhere. Go in the house." He reached for her arm and pulled the opposite way.

Faith couldn't believe her eyes. Here she was standing in front of this nigga with a newborn baby, and he was doing a complete 180 flip. Ryan was never so disrespectful, nor was he ever inconsiderate about her feelings. Within a matter of weeks, it was like all his love was lost in the wind of Mt. Everest.

"I'm sorry, Faith. You just gotta calm down and be easy," DJ mumbled before following Precious inside.

Feeling a tear about to fall, Faith quickly grabbed it with the tip of her finger before Ryan turned back around to confront her.

"Obviously you don't understand the reason I came out to Philly. This was for you all's safety. You know what I do to survive, Faith. I told you that I'm not ready to put that on pause. Not even for you. You need to go back to Delaware and stay put. You shouldn't be down here. I'll come get Prince tomorrow and we can talk then. Besides that, I have nothing else to say." Ryan folded his arms in anger.

Looking down at her baby, Faith shook her head, and released the pain she held inside. "If I knew that you were gonna be this way, I would've never allowed you to get me pregnant. You made it seem like we was just about to be this ole happy-ass family, but you with a whole 'nother female out here in Philadelphia, nigga."

"She's not my girl. Precious is my business partner."

Laughing with tears falling down her cheeks, Faith pulled the blanket around little Prince tighter. "Business, huh?"

"Yes, business, and if you can pull your head out of your ass, you'll be able to see that. Get off of my doorstep," he spat before walking inside of his crib and slamming the door.

Feeling her heart melt to pieces, Faith sucked up the sticky emotions and turned to leave. Jumping back in the car with her mother, she turned and faced her with disgust. "I don't know what to do, Mama. I love him so much. What am I gonna do about Prince?" she cried silently.

"I'm gonna tell you. We're gonna raise my little grandson to the best of our abilities and push on. We come from a family of strong black women, Faith. Where do you think you got your name? If your grandmother was still alive, she would've slapped you senseless for even dropping a tear over this selfish fool. Suck it up, princess, because your mama gonna ride with you until the damn wheels fall off," Ms. Anderson stressed before pulling off into the busy street.

* * *

After making his way inside of the living room with Precious and DJ, Ryan sat on the couch in think mode. Faith was a main concern in his mind, but how could he do his job if she wouldn't let him earn the paper like a man supposed to? Nothing could compare to the hustle of an ambitious man who wanted to take care of his fam. It was either eat or be eaten. But where was the trust?

"Are you okay?" DJ asked, passing him a lit blunt.

"Nigga, I don't want that shit. You know I get paranoid when I'm on weed. I can't think right. What is with that dumb-ass shit that Faith just pulled? All I wanna do is take care of my son. I've done too much dirt to have her creeping around this shit like this. If a nigga find out that she's my baby mama, her and my son may be taking a dirt nap in the nearest river by next week," Ryan stressed with a pissed expression. His fists were clenched tightly.

"Don't worry, bro. I promise a nigga will not lay a finger on Faith or my nephew. That's on my life. But right now, you got a bigger problem on your hands. How are we gonna move all this weight?" DJ questioned.

"I'm still lost?"

Precious sat quietly on the living room floor with a plate of Chinese chicken on her lap. She wasn't trying to ease into the conversation, but she couldn't help herself. "Did you say weight?"

Ryan and DJ looked over at her at the same time.

"What? I was just asking. I don't mean to jump in y'all business." She shrugged.

"Yeah, we talking about weight, not sugar, ma. This is really not your cup of tea." Ryan dismissed her question quickly.

"Maybe it is my cup of tea," she shot back quickly.

DJ raised an eyebrow in suspicion. "You do know what weight means, right?"

"Uh, yeah. Coke, if I'm not mistaken," Precious answered nonchalantly.

Standing up from the couch, Ryan walked over to her. "Fill me in. I'd love to hear all that you know."

Setting her plate on the coffee table, she wiped her hands with a paper napkin. "Quarters, halves, wholes, Grams, cookies, bricks. It's more of a song."

Looking at DJ with a smile, Ryan laughed. "Did you learn that from a Gucci Mane song or something?"

"Nope, my uncle."

"And I suppose your uncle is a nerdy chemist from the suburbs, right?" DJ asked with a light chuckle.

"Nope. He's an ex-drug dealer from Wilmington. His name is Lucci," she replied before pulling out her new business plans for Club Royal.

Hearing the name, Ryan paused before leaning forward on the couch. "Lucci? You mean Lucci Bruno, the Italian from the nineties who murdered the cop in front of the courthouse?"

"Yes."

"Wait, hold the fuck up. Lucci Bruno was one of the biggest dealers in Wilmington before anybody made a name for themselves out here. That's your uncle?" DJ speculated.

"Yes," Precious repeated with a smile.

"The last time I heard about him was on the news when I was a child." Ryan rose to his feet before folding his arms. "He was never seen again after that. How is this Italian related to you?"

"He's my mom's half-brother. Same father. Different mother. I'm very close to him and I spent a lot of time in my past summers with him in New York learning things about his family business, things that the average sixteen-year-old shouldn't be learning." She blushed with excitement.

"Well damn. There's your answer right there, my nigga. You got a whole suburb girl on your team who happens to be related to one of the most notorious mob bosses on uptown. Tell me you're not lucky, motherfucker." DJ shook his head in amazement.

"I want you to introduce me," Ryan spoke with seriousness.

"That's nothing. All I have to do is call in advance. He will do anything for me. "

"Now that's great timing. We need to do that as soon as possible." DJ rubbed his hands together excitedly.

"No, I need to get my team together first. This isn't an average dude." Ryan walked over to window. His mind was racing. "Do you wanna take a ride with me to the east side today?" He glanced over to his best friend.

"Of course. What do we got to lose?" DJ smiled.

Stepping over to Precious with a sinister grin, Ryan kissed her forehead twice. "I need you to stay here until I get back. Can you do that?

"Sure." She grinned with a tone of pleasure. "What's your plan?"

Pondering before he responded, Ryan grabbed his coat. "I'm going to gather the best team to ensure that we all win. It's time for a family reunion."

Chris Green

Chapter 3

East side of Delaware; the slums

Pulling his car down the polluted neighborhood, Ryan and DJ looked around at the unfamiliar faces. It was more like a zombie section of the city. The drugs were fluent, and most of the residents were either junkies or killers. There was a mutual understanding that no one could cross sections in the city unless you had a reason. A valuable reason.

"This shit looks like a deathtrap," DJ spoke with uncertainty as they turned down the one way street.

Men walked about nonchalantly with guns by their side, and all attention was focused on the expensive whip that pushed smoothly down their street.

"It's good. We can't turn around now. Just be prepared for the worst in case these niggas have ill intentions," Ryan replied before stopping in front of a three-bedroom home.

Six men who occupied the parking lot wasted no time with surrounding the car. "Are you fools lost? Y'all might got the wrong section." A dark-skinned man who sported a hoodie mugged them while eyeing the luxury car.

DJ cocked his pistol with a stern face before Ryan rolled down his window. "Nah, we in the right spot. I'm looking for Torey."

Lowering his head to look at Ryan's face, he grinned. "And you are?"

"His fucking cousin. Tell him it's important."

Pulling out a cell phone, the man stepped to the side and placed a call.

The remaining men continued to gawk at the car with a look of evilness in their movements.

After a minute passed, the man stepped back over to the car with a light smirk. "A little homage will be accepted, if you get my drift."

Reaching in his center console, Ryan grabbed a handful of hundred dollar bills, counting out two thousand bucks. He slapped it in the man's palm with a chuckle. "That's my number with it also, my nigga. Tell him my club is hosting an event tomorrow. Be there, or I'll be pulling back down here by myself."

Nodding with a respectful gesture, the man removed his hoodie. "That sounds like a plan, Mr. Delaware. The name is Free. I'll give you a call if that's accepted. Just a little advice for you. This isn't the north side. Try not to appear without permission."

"I am the permission. Either he comes, or I'll be back. Remember. This is only the east side, not the murder capital." Ryan rolled up his window and pulled gently away from the curb.

Making their way out of the blocked-in street, DJ took a deep breath. "Don't ever do that shit again to me. I was about to kill that nigga. We can't just talk like that to these folks, bro."

"We can do whatever the fuck we want. We run Wilmington, not the east side. Without us, there is no air. I'll kill everybody, even my cuz, if an ounce of our blood gets shed. Thank Raekwon for that." Ryan grinned with assurance. "Do you remember the last nigga my dad popped before he left?"

Thinking hard, DJ glanced over to him. "No."

"Let's just say that we saved a few niggas. Men who were supposed to be killed with no mercy. That east side miracle came from the hands of a north side man. A miracle that these fools live by today. My dad rescued a person that these idiots worshipped. His new foundation was building a road to respect for men where we come from. A tradition that won't be broken for one reason," Ryan spoke while keeping his eyes on the road.

"Why?"

"Family.

"Cheek." DJ smirked.

"Exactly."

* * *

Wilmington detention facility

After walking up the small steps for the attorney booth, Cheek Raw opened the door and locked eyes with Detective Christopher Bradley. Flashing him a look of hate, he snatched up the phone. "It seems like I can't get a phone to be answered after this whole agreement. Is there a reason my young nigga went missing in action?"

"You know why, Cheek. It's clear. "

"Motherfucker, you said that he wouldn't get a chance to be in that position. I haven't even did my ties with the table. All that work I put in! I haven't even met the cartel. This is a family organization. You can't just move off of your own rules, motherfucker."

Giving him a pathetic look, Bradley yawned. "I've never made the rules, Raw. I just enforce them. You are the one who decided to run the streets with a mission on winning the entire world over with your arrogant press. You played yourself out of position, and now you have to fix it through him. "

Titling his head, Cheeks snarled into the receiver. "So what the fuck you saying?"

"I'm saying that you've been voted off. The table has to move on without you, and of course it leads down to the rookie you decided to bring along. "

"I'm not about to place the fate of my position in this young bull. You know what his reputation is about. Ryan is a loose cannon. You setting me up for failure, Bradley. I got twenty-five years to do, mother-fucker!"

"And hopefully it will do you some good. I warned you about the dumb shit. You didn't comply, and now you're facing the consequences. Open your eyes, Raw, this is your last hope to save yourself. It's either him or you, choose one," Bradley ordered. He picked at his nails while sitting back in the chair, waiting for an answer.

Slamming the phone receiver across the glass, Cheek Raw rose to his feet. His voice boomed. "Bull-shit! I ain't allowing you to get over on me with no shit like that. My word overrules yours, nigga!"

"Not anymore, dumbass. As the enforcer of the ta-ble, I'm in control of your seat. You must forgot who brought you to this bitch! Without me, you wouldn't have even known about the input your father shared with this organization. Your father was from the east, and unfortunately, this isn't an eastside chair. I'm run-ning the north side and I say that Ryan will pick up where you left off. If he succeeds, than that will be great on your part, but if he fails, then you fail," Brad-ley warned before standing to his feet to leave. "Oh yeah, before I forget. Try to keep your mouth closed about this discussion. We don't need Ryan fumbling because of you feeding him nonsense. Your spot will resume after you finish your time. It's either that, or a permanent sleep."

"Whatever you say, slime-ass motherfucker. Just to let you know, I'm not gonna lose, and there are also ways around you. People I know that you can't reach, Bradley. So have your fun while it lasts, pussy, 'cause it won't be this way for long. "

Bradley couldn't help but smile. "One false move, and you could lose it all. Why take chances?" he asked with a devilish grin before exiting the attorney visit room.

* * *

24 hours later
Club Royal
10:01 p.m.

Things were glowing in the midst of Club Royal tonight. Not only was it a special day to win, but it was also the night of an official takeover. Money was the mission. It was a moment to be relentless and crush the game into his palm. That was all Ryan could think about as he posted in the VIP sectional of his small business. The music boomed through the walls, and women flooded the floors with their crushes of the night.

DJ tapped Ryan's shoulder lightly. "Do you really think this nigga coming?"

"Who can deny money, bro? It's no reason to start friction when you can eat like a true thorough man should. Sometimes we just gotta have a little patience." Ryan paused his speech and nodded towards the entrance of his club.

DJ glanced over the small wall at a dark-skinned man who stood still by the double doors, watching him make contact towards their section. He slid through the dance floor. He quickly mixed in with the medium-sized crowd until reaching his destination.

Removing the hoodie from his head, he climbed the small five stairs and locked eyes with Ryan. "If it ain't true, it ain't you. What it do, fool?" He flashed an evil grin at his cousin.

Ryan rose to his feet with a wide smirk. "Took you long enough. I didn't think my blood was sacred no more."

They embraced in a small hug. They both chuckled.

"This is my partner in crime, DJ. DJ, this is Torey," Ryan introduced the two.

"Wassup, my dude?" DJ reached out his hand to the stranger.

Torey nodded instead of accepting his gesture. "None much, my dude."

Ryan looked down in DJ's eyes and could tell that he was offended by the action. Instead of replying, he reached for his drink and began to vibe with the booming beat.

"So what brings me out to the north side on such short notice? I haven't seen you since my mama's funeral." Torey pulled a blunt from his left pants pockets.

Ryan touched his shoulder and examined his family. He had to admit that the young cousin he remembered from years ago was growing tremendously fast. His little twists were now a head full of dreadlocks. The peach fuzz on his chin was now a full-grown beard. Still and all, he possessed those same dark black demon eyes. It was the look of a man who didn't fear, the one who didn't require a soul to live. It was an expression he wore perfectly.

"You're here because I need you. Things is hard for me right now, and I figured that you could offer me some advice with a few things. For old time's sake," Ryan stressed before folding his arms.

Twirling up a nice joint, Torey sparked it with a small Bic lighter. "Old time's sake? I missed you, Ryan, but I don't kill for fun anymore." He blew a cloud of smoke from his nostrils.

"No doubt, but that's not what I mean, family. We never was able to link with a little business. I'm pushing now."

Laughing, Torey stared in his eyes. "Nigga, you know damn well I'm not a worker. We've been through this before, Ryan."

"The only nigga you working for is yourself." Ryan stretched his arm to point around his entire establishment. "All this came from dealing with the right people who know the right things. It was a chance I took, cuz. I'm looking for you to help me build. This is a gig that'll put us in position within a few months."

"Ain't we all trying to build, Ryan? I've been pressed to be this way. Every time I switched up my flow, it was for the cause of another nigga. My patience don't live there no more." Torey shrugged his shoulders. His facial expression confirmed the little interest from his cousin's conversation.

"I'm not just any nigga, Torey. In fact, I'm not in the same category as these fools. I'm family. Treat me accordingly. There hasn't been one time that you've recorded me in that mind of yours doing anything against the grain. That should warm you up on giving me a shot. We've had situations, but you've never seen me ask for help. This is big." Ryan sounded more desperate than arrogant, a characteristic that Torey wasn't used to.

Looking out at the thick crowd, Torey clasped his hands together. "Family will let you down sometimes, Ryan, but me never having bad business with you is a true statement. I know where to find you." He lightly mushed Ryan's shoulder with a smile.

"I hope so," Ryan mumbled while watching his cousin ease back through the moving club. The time was perfected accordingly, and it was positive on what Ryan's next move was. In order for shit to flourish, you had to accept someone. A team wasn't just one person. It was a group of individuals that were chosen by one person with a vision.

Looking back at DJ with a smile, Ryan raised his glass of coconut Ciroc. "It looks like we in effect, bro."

"Good. Let's just be sure we doing the right thing," DJ replied with sincerity written on his face.

"There ain't no other way." Ryan grinned before chugging his drink. His mind could see the dough that was about to touch his hands. Nothing was about to block the path of that. Not even family.

Chapter 4

The loud band music sounded off as the director of the school recited the high school graduate names of 2019. The gymnasium was packed to the fullest capacity, and the red caps and gowns covered the entire stage.

After hearing DJ's name boom through the microphone, half of the building erupted with applause. Not only was DJ one of the most popular attending, but he was also the smartest, topping the grade average list of Newark High. He was guaranteed a scholarship to Princeton University and a bright future with his literature skills. He would be the first to gain a successful life out of Wilmington, Delaware for sure.

"That's my nigga!" Ryan jumped to his feet and clapped loudly.

Flashing everyone in the crowd a bright thirty-two, DJ walked across the stage and grabbed his diploma.

The sight of his best friend grabbing that certificate placed a giant lock on Ryan's heart. It was a promise that DJ made to him in middle school. All he ever spoke on was completing high school and becoming one of the best magazine owners the world had ever seen. His skills for writing were beyond exceptional. From competitions to college course essays, he would always be number one on the list. It gave him the motivation to push further and move up for his own publishing company. That vision was prospering quickly, and now the time for celebration was here.

Ryan snapped a quick photo of DJ as he stopped for a picture with the school principal. It was an unforgettable day that he loved and regretted at the same time. All he had to do was complete one last school year, and he would've crossed the same stage as his best friend, succeeding together. But the streets had possession over his flesh, and Ryan's heart just didn't see that path feeding his son at the time. A diploma didn't feed your stomach at night when your bank account was on zero. A job sounded pretty good until it was time for that rent to be paid. The quick way was another rush, one that'd set you straight for life. That was all Ryan wanted.

After watching the entire school cross the stage, he listened to Faith's name ring through the speakers. All he could do was look at her beautiful ass stroll across the stage with confidence. She ensured Ryan that school was the main priority, and that was the reason his respect flew a thousand miles high for her. Even though she couldn't understand his position with the streets, there wasn't a day that passed where he didn't consider that wish for the sake of his family. Being the sole provider caused him to see shit differently. It was upon the man to take care of home. Even if the woman tried to object. A real man would die before he held out his hand to another nigga. It felt horrible to watch that tragic problem fall over Ryan's home. Still, it wouldn't stop him from chasing that paper for his son's well-being.

After the ceremony was complete, the entire event poured out into the lobby, where everyone hugged their graduates. Mothers and fathers took pictures with the administration of the school, and the teen girls moved around screaming at every damn female friend they probably were never gonna see again.

Ryan made his way through the crowd, shaking hands with the familiar faces from school, until he crossed DJ's family. "Nigga, you did it." He smiled at his friend with an ecstatic expression

DJ couldn't help but to embrace him. "I couldn't have done it without your help, my nigga. All them days you convinced me not to quit. Man, this shit was hard." He laughed while holding up his high school diploma.

"Man, it wasn't hard. You just had to keep your dream in mind. That shit can't build without you finishing, ya know. "

Nodding, DJ folded his arms. "I really wish you could have walked across with us, bro. That hurt me even worse when I heard them call Wicked's name."

Thinking about his remark, Ryan quickly flushed those feelings and changed the subject. "Guess what, bro? I'ma be good no matter what I do, and I know Wicked will touch down and handle his business on gaining access to that big boy certificate right there. In the end, I'm just glad to see you prosper," he explained before wrapping his arm around DJ's neck. "Tonight is on me, so what do you wanna do?"

Cheesing from all the hundred dollar bills that Ryan was pulling out of his left pocket, DJ shrugged. "Shittt, I'm down for whatever."

Before they could make an exit, Ryan's eyes landed on Faith and Markie D standing in front of him. By the look on her face, he knew that she was about to land a fist full of questions about this and that. It surely wasn't the right time, especially with the way Markie D was flashing his fake-ass daddy savior mug.

Before Ryan could speak, DJ tapped him lightly on the chest. "Don't get mad, bro. Just give her five minutes to talk with you and let it be. Remember, we kicking shit tonight, not getting mad," he whispered before bending a quick U-turn.

Approaching Ryan, Faith gave him the dirtiest look ever. Her hand instantly moved to slap him across the face, but he quickly grabbed her wrist.

"Girl, what the hell is your problem!"

"How could you be sitting here huddling up with your friend on the day of my graduation? You didn't even congratulate me!"

Balling up his face in anger, Ryan pushed her hand down. "Because of problems like this, Faith. I'm not accepting that immature shit anymore. You're the reason I don't wanna be around. You don't know how to act."

A few graduates and families glanced their way, eyes wide like they were waiting for some family drama shit to pop off.

Markie D stepped in between them. "This is not the spot for y'all to be doing this. Gain some sense of this situation now, and remember that y'all ain't the only ones who can show ya ass in here." His voice was humble, but thick.

Out of respect for the old head, Ryan took a small step back. "This ain't what I came here for. Your daughter is stepping out of boundaries with the way she's been acting, so maybe y'all need to talk with her. I'm grown, and nobody around this motherfucker is my parent."

"You may be right, son, but let me tell you something." Markie D closed the small space between them. "I was around when you was just a tiny child. The respect for your father was mutual, young bull. This is still my daughter. You're absolutely right. I'm not your father. But I know Raekwon, and you wouldn't be treating my daughter like this if he was around."

"Fuck him, Daddy. Let's just go. He ain't nothing but a drug dealer anyway," Faith spat.

Chuckling, Ryan waved them both off. "Look, Markie, no disrespect, you should've raised ya child better. Until she fixes her act, I'll be taking care of my son from a distance."

"And that's fine, Ryan. I'm not gonna push you to come around this family if you're not willing, but I didn't ask you to get my daughter pregnant."

"Neither did I, but it happened. It seems like we have this same problem every time we cross each other's path. From now on, I'll send my child's money through Ms. Anderson. Stress is the last thing I need around me, and I'm not going to win if she wanna nag for all the smallest reasons," Ryan stated before turning to walk away.

Markie D couldn't help but to look down into his daughter's hurt face. Her eyes began to slowly tear up, and that was something he refused to see her do on her special day. "Let's go, baby girl. You have to always remember, if a man don't want you, he'll express it through his actions. Then it will reach his tongue. Once it spills from his mouth, there's nothing left to fight for but pain, Faith." He draped his arm around her neck and turned the opposite way.

Accepting her father's harsh but true words, she removed her graduation cap before they could exit the school's side door.

Ryan made his way swiftly back to where DJ stood with a few of their home room classmates. Embracing a few of the graduates with a handshake, he playfully punched DJ in the chest. "So what's it gonna be, nigga? How we wildin' out tonight, Club, house party?"

Smiling, DJ flipped his graduation banner like the collar of a Delaware player. "I wanna lay up in the crib with a few lady friends. Eat a little, drink some apple juice, and smoke all the weed I can. "

Laughing, Ryan tossed him a small car key box. "How fast can you make it back to my spot?"

Staring at the cat symbol on the black square, DJ smirked. "That depends on who gets across the bridge first."

Ryan formed a devilish smirk before they both jogged quickly out of Newark High.

* * *

Reckless, 5th and Monroe

The block was burning hot with all the police cruisers that pushed around. It was always the same on Tuesdays and Thursdays. It was payday for the fiends, and jump-out day for the pigs. Still through all the calamity and envy, Reckless managed to keep that early bird mentality in his system. If you didn't put in the action to lay on a sweet lick, you would probably end up kicking in doors for flat screens and furniture sets. That was a move Reckless intended on staying far away from. You could be the toughest nigga in the state, but if the money was good enough, yo' ass was got.

He cut his eyes to the SUV that was pulling down the street. It came to a halt directly in front of him. The passenger side window began to lower, releasing a thick cloud of marijuana smoke. Moving off his instincts, Reckless clutched on his strap.

"If you don't know what block you on, I suggest you swerve this piece of shit down the street!

"Damn, young one. Calm down. It's surprising to see you out here on this block moving alone with an attitude like that." Severe opened the car door and stepped out.

The sight of his face made Reckless wanna pull on his trigger. Even though the beef was personal with him and Ryan, it was natural to feel hatred for a nigga who tried to plot against someone you were close to. Wrinkling up his nose, Reckless glanced at the three men who were occupying the vehicle. "I move where I want to, and I don't need nobody when I got a full seventeen on my hip. Any specific reason why you worried about me?"

Severe raised his hands in peace. "Why you so negative, young blood? I'm not a talkative person, and you know that it's only one way I handle my problems. Getting out of my car to have this fake-ass conversation ain't one. I'm here to speak my business and leave." His posture was calm, and the way he leaned against his car caused Reckless to ease his tension.

"What conversation do we need to have? I don't owe you nothing, and I surely don't know you besides the recent shit you had going on with Ryan. Doesn't seem like it's nothing to talk about." Reckless shrugged.

Shaking his head, Severe approached him slowly. "Listen, I don't know if you're aware of this or not, but Delaware is the smallest city around the entire north.

Shit float around like air in the sky, and anything the streets know makes it everybody's business. Like that dumb-ass move you and Wicked pulled with them clowns on the south side. "

"I don't know what the fuck you're talking about." Reckless glared into his eyes without blinking.

Smirking, Severe exhaled deeply. "Sure you don't. It's not my business on finding out if you did or not. I really don't give a fuck at all, if you wanna be honest. The hood knows what Wicked is locked up for. I'm just being a good street nigga and passing the word on. My team won't pass up no paperwork, but we also ain't accepting no dummy missions. We could use a young bull like you on the team. It's better than getting pushed out the way by your own crew," Severe said with seriousness lacing his tone.

"As I said the first time, Ryan is the least of my problems. If he was really looking for me, I would've been found. This block ain't changing no time soon, buddy. It's just me and my friend, so I'll be ready." Reckless patted the gun on his hip.

"Yeah, yeah. You'll be ready, and nobody gonna step wrong," Severe mumbled sarcastically. "I hear all that and truly I'm not knocking none of it, but when your name ringing in the east and south side, we have a problem. If you ever change your mind, you know where to find me. "

Reckless watched Severe as he climbed back in the passenger seat of the vehicle and slowly pulled off. The slick comment caused his nerves to slightly rattle. Ryan was surely mad and in his feelings about some sissy shit in Reckless's eyes. Real friends never folded when it came down to whatever situation. You could never get the loyalty from a true homeboy back, especially when the root of money was in between the equation. In the end, it didn't matter. There was only one way things were ending. Come correct, kill, or be killed, and go against any nigga that wasn't rocking with him or Wicked. Nothing else mattered. Eventually Ryan would have to cross paths with him to give the clarification on how things would escalate, and that day would determine who was built to last, because one or the other would die wherever they stood.

* * *

9 hours later
Ryan's spot, Philly, Cedar Street

The loud Meek Mill song that was pounding through Ryan's speakers had everyone amped to the max. The graduation from Newark was not only the best thing that happened for the attendants of the party, but Ryan's surprise for them was gonna be forever memorable. DJ played a major role in the mix of his new business, and accomplishing his high school diploma made things even better. Smoke was filling the air from the loud weed and bottles were being flipped like a bad-ass channel. It was a moment for celebration. A few people didn't know that they were invited for a purpose. It was all Ryan could think of since they all crossed his threshold. It was the perfect team.

Heading back over to the circle where DJ stood, Ryan raised a cold bottle of Pinnacle vodka. "This the last of it. If we need any more, then one of these li'l hoochies gotta stroll. "

DJ couldn't help but to laugh. "We shouldn't need anything else after all this damn liquor we just consumed. It feels good to be free from Newark, bro. I just wanna run me up some money to pay off my college courses. I got nine months to kick some shit before I take off. "

"That's the last thing you need to worry about, bro. We eating with this shit. Tomorrow we dropping this shit off and putting the plan in place. I've estimated the numbers, and you'll have enough money to pay off your school fees with extra. That's the reason I called everybody to my spot today. All these niggas who here gonna play a part in what we have going on. You got Nas." Ryan pointed over towards the kitchen where a brown-skinned man was posted against the wall. "He's from the south side. Not only is his dad tied in with the dope boys, but his smart skills for counting will help us also. Over there by the front door is Freddie. He's from the west side. A lot of our connections and clientele will come through him. He's in the loop with some important people, and I'm not taking about the average cocaine dealer in Wilmington. It's a blessing when ya mama can come home and tell you about the last three people she sentenced to a long trip down prison alley. Judging ain't all she good with either." Ryan sipped his bottle while nodding to the music.

"How did you find out all this?" DJ asked in a slurred tone.

Smirking with an evil grin, Ryan shrugged his shoulders. "I have my ways. But that's not important right now. All I want you to do is enjoy the night, and get ready for our take-off tomorrow. We ain't gotta do nothing but distribute and watch the money pile like dirty laundry."

Nodding, DJ pulled on the sour diesel. He looked around at all the teens having the time of their lives. He envisioned what his life was about to be like when those college doors opened up for him. This was a new foundation to build for his career and family. It was the last thing that he wanted to mess up by slipping around in the streets of Wilmington. "I ain't gonna even lie, Ryan. I'm ready and all, bro, but I don't need nothing to mess this up for me. My mom is counting on this and I - "

"DJ, you don't have to explain yourself, bro. I'm not gonna let you down, and I know what this means to yo' mama too. I'm not about to waste time anymore. Early in the a.m., we dropping shit off, and placing it all in motion. You're gonna have that paycheck in no time for them good Negro scamming-ass people. I sent a little sample out and seen the paper within the next hour. That was in Philly, not Wilmington. We're good fa'sho." Ryan grinned before wrapping an arm around his neck.

Nodding with a small smile, DJ remained quiet. His mind wanted to speak on different things, but he didn't want to kill the vibe of everyone at the small bash. He surely didn't want Ryan to think that he was bailing out either. Gaining that scholarship to one of the best colleges in the United States proved to him that his dreams could be the new way to feed his fam, especially after his mom placed her all into getting him through school. Instead of speaking his feelings, DJ tucked them underneath his sleeve and decided to go with the flow. There was only nine months before school started, and he was gonna be sure to make it front and center by any means necessary. "So what about Torey?" He snapped out of his trance and took a swig of his strong cup.

"Torey is a nigga who likes press, and I'm the one to do it. He's my cousin, but I'm sure we will be able to come down to an understanding. This city has been dry for years without a real supplier. Supreme was the last hope, and you see how that turned out. This is the easiest thing that we will be able accomplish. It's us against the world, bro."

Demerea pulling on Ryan's hand and stopped him in mid-sentence. "Are you too busy for a quick convo?" She blushed with a polite expression. Her firm body was looking magnificent in her two piece Versace sweat suit. Her makeup was past sufficient, and her hair was braided to the back with a highlight of honey blonde at the tips.

Looking her up and down, Ryan grabbed her hand, and forced her to do a small spin. "Demerea? What the hell happened to you overnight, girl?"

She was all smiles. It was rare to get a remark from him, so she wanted that moment to last as long as it could, "Oh stop it, Ry, this just my little graduation set up. I feel great. I'm finally free from Newark High, and now I can go on to be one of the baddest bitches to succeed at whatever I choose. "

"You sure you ain't at the wrong party? Them tight-ass pants got that ass sitting on 26's. The stripper party ain't until after midnight." DJ laughed.

She flicked him a finger. She looked back at Ryan, who gazed at her quietly. "Dang, boy. Why you drooling? You know Faith bound to pop up and spazz on you."

"Please." He twisted up his face like that was an insult. "Faith don't run me. I'm just looking. Ain't no harm in that."

"Nah, it ain't. I needed to talk to you though. I know you busy with this little get together or whatever, but I can make it quick."

Looking around at his surroundings, Ryan locked eyes with DJ before turning back to Demerea. "Come on. We can just go to my room."

Sliding through the crowd, Ryan led her to the back of his apartment, stepping into the master bedroom.

She giggled. "Who the hell decorated your room? It looks like Kimyetta slid through here, boy."

"I know that's right. My mama's ass been missing ever since my pop been gone. This my flavor right here. Everything handpicked by me." Ryan chuckled, flopping down on his king-sized bed. "But wassup though?"

Her eyes couldn't help but to roll down towards his print. "Umm. I know you really a secretive person with the way you move or whatever, but I'm about to get a new job at this strip joint in New York. I know for a fact that I can get you some clientele out of Brooklyn for sure."

Raising up off the bed, Ryan stared at her suspiciously. "Clientele? I don't know what you're talking about."

Smacking her lips. She placed a hand on her hip. "Boy, you know that niggas' lips run like a leaky faucet around this city. I know what you do, Ryan, so don't try and treat me like I'm a new girl. I'm digging the movement, and I wanna help you run the dough up too. Is there any harm in that?" she asked seductively with her ass poking extra hard for his attention.

Her shape was polluting his eyesight because that ass was surely getting phat. Her luscious lips and cheeks were a plus with the bomb mascara that aligned her eyelids. She was smelling like a bucket of berries, and her damn coochie print glowed like a number one trophy inside the thin, tight-cutting fabric she wore.

"Nah, ain't no harm in that, but my business shouldn't be getting spoken on from no one if it ain't me. You ain't been trying to get down with no trap game, so what's the catch, Demerea?"

"There is none. I know you a real one. I don't want to seem like I'm on some thirsty shit, especially when Faith has been running around thinking everybody is out to get you. I'm in it to see your pockets get bigger - and of course mines. I'm just willing to put in work instead of asking for anything," she admitted.

Nodding, Ryan stood up and stepped closer to her. He was so close that she could smell the Axe body wash pumping from his skin.

"You ain't been trying to get on my team. Why the sudden change of heart?" He was breathing down her neck like a dog in heat.

The liquor smell on his breath ensured her that he was past tipsy, and the inside of her panties couldn't help but to indulge with his flirtatious movements. That cookie was twitching, and if he wasn't careful, she was gonna wrap his little nose up the crack of her ass. She knew the pussy could cross his vision like a line between two dots, and her opportunity to make herself relevant was surely approaching. Instead of giving him a full treat, Demerea decided to play his game.

"You know that I'm that chick, boy. Ain't none of these thotiana-ass bitches in the ranks to be on no gutta shit like me. Maybe I see the same in you. I would rather be with a solid one before I go out bad with a nigga who ain't built like that. Like I said, I want some dough," she said arrogantly.

Gripping a handful of her petite ass, Ryan lightly bit into the side of her neck and slid his tongue down to her shoulder blade.

Moaning lightly, she scratched his back. "Ryan, you need to be careful. You drunk, and you feeling yourself. Don't get hurt." She smiled with a sneaky grin.

"I'm not that drunk. I know that you in my room talking shit right now. We could've been done by now." He smirked, still holding a handful of her booty.

"I see you just not gonna stop tonight, huh?"

"Not if you don't want me to."

In one swift motion, she pulled his stiff manhood from the blue Robin jeans he wore, swirling a finger down his stomach. Demerea bent down and gazed up into his eyes before taking him deep into her mouth.

Ryan grabbed the back of her head, guiding her to a perfect rhythm. She started to handle the business like a true porn star. Her mouth flooded with saliva as she gagged from the force of his shit touching her tonsils.

"Mmmm." She swirled her tongue in a circular motion while taking him down.

Biting his bottom lip, Ryan began to rock his hips back and forth. Demerea wasn't playing with the head game, and she wanted to prove a point. If you was fucking with her, then you obviously was fucking with the best. It didn't take long before she felt his muscles tightening up. Without stopping, she drank every drop he offered. She flicked her tongue out as if she was a good child eating all her vegetables.

"Damn, I guess you really is about that issue, huh?" He was breathing heavily from the load he busted.

"You haven't seen nothing." She pulled down her sweats to show him a glimpse of her smooth brown cheeks. Her plump kitty lips could be seen from the back, and the freaky gesture caused his young man to raise back up.

Licking his fingers, he placed them in the crack of her butt. "This looks good, and I wanna try it."

"Mm-hmm." Sliding away from his touch, she pulled her clothes back up. "Maybe when I know that you ain't just finna treat me like I'm one of your other sluts. If I get that dick in me, I want it for good." She smiled before leaning down to kiss his hard rod. "Who knows? After business flows, we might fuck so good that it'll bring us a baby."

"Oh, it's like that, huh?" Ryan pulled up his jeans in satisfaction.

"Only until you make it different," she shot back.

Before she could leave out his bedroom door, he grabbed ahold of her arm.

* * *

The loud doorbell caused DJ to raise his head out of the young girl's breasts. "Damn, can somebody get the door?" he screamed out over the music.

Turning back around to his little cutie, he began to fondle her shirt. The bell sounded again, causing him to exhale deeply. "Excuse me for a second, li'l mama," he whispered before turning around to catch the guest.

The sight of everybody lingering around loudly forced DJ to shake his head. Motherfuckers would turn into full zombies when it came to the right drugs. People were dancing in circles to music that was meant for a fucking wedding so it was clear on who was wasted and blitzed to the limit.

Reaching the door, DJ snatched it open and stared Precious in her face. He looked at the large bag of McDonald's she held. He forced a phony-ass smile. "Heyyy, what's good, Precious?"

"Hey DJ, is Ryan in?" She looked over his shoulder with a curious grin.

Blocking her sight off quickly, he stuttered. "Uh, yeah, but it think he's using the bathroom."

"Good." Precious slid past him into the apartment, running into the crowd of guests. She looked back at DJ. "Is it someone's birthday?"

"Nah. Today was just our graduation. We got a few people together and kicked it," he replied. The only thing that crossed his mind was Ryan and Demerea. A slip up like this was gonna be one that he could never come back from.

Just as she began to move through the crowd, DJ spotted the two coming from the back room. He watched as Precious made her way over to him. "Hey Ryan. I got good news for you." She pulled him in for a hug before he could reject.

Demerea mugged her with a nasty frown before smacking her lips. "Uhh, Ryan, if you don't mind, please call me when it's time to handle that. I'm in need of it," she mentioned before rolling her eyes and walking off.

"What got her panties in a bunch?" Precious asked with a raised eyebrow.

"Don't worry about her. She just trying to do some business for another clientele in Delaware. Unfortunately, I ain't taking no new friends, so that's been placed on the back burner. Wassup with you?" He grinned at how good she was looking.

Precious was just that type of girl every man could love. Her beauty was like none other, not to mention her apple bottom always hugged the inside of her pants like a magnet. She was one that couldn't be ratchet even if she tried. Her brilliant side was always a shocker to Ryan, but it seemed like he adored her more with every moment she spent around him. He knew for a fact that she would be a true best friend for life.

"I'm good." She looked into his eyes with a slight smirk. "Ryan, are you drunk?"

Laughing, he grabbed her warm hands and placed them under his shirt. She could feel his muscles and a steady heartbeat pumping through his chest. "Am I warm or cold?"

"Uh, you're pretty warm to me." She snickered, feeling a tingle flush through her skin.

"Good, that means I'm not drunk yet," he said before walking over to the loud stereo system, flicking off the switch. The entire room complained in unison. "Listen, listen. This get together has been a good one, and I'm grateful that you all came to chill with us for this last time. I'm glad that most of y'all was able to make it out of Newark, but y'all gotta tear it down. Party is over," Ryan announced.

"Damn, man, this shit was just getting good!" he heard a man yell out.

"Exactly. You don't need too much fun. You gotta think about how you about to make some bread now, 'cause that school excuse is dead," DJ said before opening the front door. "Get to stepping, and clear this shit out." He clapped his hands with a gigantic smile.

Watching the living room slowly evacuate, Ryan grabbed a trash bag and began to pick up the excess trash that laid on the floor. After everyone dispersed, the only people who lingered around were Nas and Freddie. The purpose of the party was for one cause, and now the time was being presented to lay the cards out on the table.

"If y'all don't mind, we can all come together over here to speak on what's going to happen. I'm not trying to be long, and the easiest way to explain this is being uncut and straight down to the point."

Nas, Freddie, and DJ took a seat on Ryan's living room couch as he began to break things down on how the operation would take place. After being sure of Nas and Freddie's agreement to do business, he shook hands with the men and escorted them out of the front door.

"Bright and early, gentlemen," he said before closing the door behind him.

Looking at DJ and Precious with a wide grin, Ryan rubbed his hands together. "I think we will be running the streets of Delaware within a week."

Sipping on her bottle of water, Precious nodded. "Maybe sooner."

"What makes you say that?" DJ butted in.

"Because my uncle wants to meet you," she said with a straight face.

Walking over to her, Ryan placed a juicy kiss on her lips. "You're the best friend I've ever had."

"Ryan, I'm flattered." She blushed.

"That's sounds good, but when does he want to get together?" DJ wanted to keep the business at mind.

"This weekend."

Chapter 5

Swerving through the streets of Delaware in his Infiniti truck, Ryan turned on the intersecting lane to reach the eastside city limits. As he cruised through the small neighborhood, he eyed all of the local bustas who watched his fly whip. It was known for Delaware niggas to beef with Philly cats back in the day, so he knew that his new license plates were definitely an eye catcher. Laughing to himself, Ryan pulled down his cousin's street and parked the car directly in front of his establishment. After killing the engine, he jumped out of the whip fresher than a pack of Mentos. The beige pea coat he wore matched the OSA skullcap on his head. His crisp Gucci white T-shirt was straight off the shelf, and the brown bleached Balenciaga jeans were a shade lighter than the wheat Timberland boots on his feet.

Free couldn't help but to make a slick remark after he stepped in the yard. "That looks like the man right there, y'all. I know this nigga came to take care of the hood."

A few armed men stood next to him looking for the best inmate mugshots to flash. It was clearly a prank, because half of the hood already knew who Ryan's father was, not to mention the work that he put in himself.

Ryan smiled and pulled out a wad of blue face hundreds, flexing them with a thumb spread. "Sorry, li'l bro. I ain't got nothing but big bills. I'll make sure to leave my cousin something for you," he replied while continuing up the driveway.

Torey appeared in the screen door once his cousin reached the porch. "If it ain't my big timer-ass family. What's good?"

"Nah, I'm just Ryan," he said before stepping inside the home.

"Blah, blah." Torey waved him off. "I'm talking about this work you gave me. Where did you find this shit?"

"What do you mean?

"That shit is nearly sold out. Ever since you dropped it off, my phone hasn't stop ringing," Torey said with a straight face.

"Bullshit. I just gave you that shit two days ago." Ryan flashed a curious grin. That comment sounded too good to be true. A kilo was bound to take the average nigga a full week to push, and that was off break down.

The sound of Torey's phone vibrating caused him to flash Ryan an "I told you so" facial expression. "First off all, I'm a taker, not a hustler. If I'm telling you something like this, it's the truth. "

"How did you get off five bricks in two days? Who the hell you selling this shit to?"

"That's not your concern, Ginuwine. All you gotta do is feed me some more. As long as I'm getting my cut, I'm good." Torey smirked.

"Cool. How much do you want?

"How much do you think can fit in that Infiniti truck?" he replied sarcastically.

Ryan thought to himself about how much money he could make in the next few days before the meeting presented itself. Reaching the quota was his only mission, so Torey's request would be answered by any means. "How about I have DJ pull up and surprise you?"

Torey headed over to his dining room table and grabbed a medium-sized tote bag from underneath it. After passing it to Ryan, he folded his arms. "It wouldn't matter to me. Just to let you know, I've never been good at being a worker. This is only gonna last for so long before I depart and do my own thing. I just wanna give you the heads up."

Ryan embraced him with a hug and handshake. "Everybody gotta have a dream, cuzzo," he responded before leaving out of the front door.

"So who you supposed to be now, Dr. King?"

Flashing a cheesy smile, Ryan shook his head. "I told you, I'm just Ryan, nigga."

After trailing back down to the parking lot, he jumped in his whip and started the engine. He looked over at Free, who sat on the side of Torey's spot with his co-signing butt buddies. Ryan flicked him a middle finger before smashing off.

The operation was better than good. It was perfect. If all fell correctly, he would off the work before the cartel called for their next meeting. Teamwork was something that Ryan wasn't used to, but it was hard not to see differently after experiencing the first few days of the business movements. Shit was lovely.

The sound of his cell ringing grasped his attention, quickly pushing that thought to the back of his mind. He picked it up and answered.

"Hello?"

"Young bull, long time no see. Where the love at?" Cheek's voice flowed through the receiver.

"Cheek?"

"The one and only. Why I gotta get a nigga to let me use a cell phone in order to get a pick up from you?"

"Nah, fool. It's not like that. I been out here in the loop, so you know how that shit go. The money calling me, big bro. Do you need something?"

"Yeah, I need to know what the hell you got going on with Detective Bradley."

Glancing down at the number on his screen to be extra careful on the way he was talking, Ryan placed his mouth back up to the receiver. "Why the hell you even mentioning dude's name on the line, old head? That's more of a personal, face to face discussion."

"Calm down, bull. This is a throwaway, not the wall phone. You must didn't open up your ears when you first answered the phone," Cheek replied a little more aggressively.

"Yo, lower your tone, Cheek. I'm not with all the arguing, my nigga. What does it matter what me and him got going on? Is there a problem?" Ryan kept his eyes on the road and placed him on speaker phone.

"Hell yeah it's a problem, nigga. You eating off my plate, and I'm not receiving shit for it. I bet he didn't tell you that you're sitting in my seat right now. You don't know what the fuck you're getting yourself into, Ryan!"

"Whoa, Cheek, pump your motherfucking brakes. You sound real crazy through the line, old head. Before you speak on anything that's dealing with me, nigga, question Bradley, not me. I never asked you for shit. I'm winning right now because I put in work. It sounds like you mad," Ryan spat.

"Young bull, you don't even have a clue. If you make the wrong move, your ass will die."

"What!" Ryan balled up his face. "Is that a threat, nigga?

"Young bull, just listen to - "

"Fuck that, nigga, it sounds like you on some real hoe shit right now," Ryan cut Cheek off quickly. "Don't call my fucking phone speaking crooked statements 'cause you ain't the only person who built like that, old head. Suck a dick, and take it easy. Instead of worrying about the money I'm making. You need to focus on the law library and not dropping that soap in the shower, pussy!" Ryan yelled before hanging up.

He slid the phone in his pocket and sat back in the driver's seat. The audacity of Cheek Raw checking him about a cop was a big insult. Not only did Ryan pave his own way, but he had never approached Bradley once. The opportunity was presented to him, and he didn't hesitate to step up with that position. The only mission was a meal ticket. No one was coming in the way of that cheese - not Kimyetta, not Cheek, not even Detective Bradley. All he needed was a check to feed Prince for good, and that would be enough for him. Life was good, and the dope game was sweet. Ryan just didn't know about the evil bitter side that could switch shit within a few seconds, bitter things that could squeeze the soul right out of your skin, leaving no room to breathe again. It was a journey that he was willing to take in order to stamp his name. He was the king of Delaware.

* * *

Tyleema's house, Newcastle, DE

"I wouldn't care who's out or in. We need to start thinking of something now, because I'm tired of letting the slick indirect threats go. I'm about to start playing for keeps," Reckless said to Tyleema as he put out his cigarette in the broken ashtray. His mind was so focused on taking Ryan out of his position that he didn't see Sekoya's car pull inside the driveway.

"Listen, Reckless. You have to be careful. We don't know what Ryan has in store or who he has protecting him. He probably has eyes on you right now," she stressed. There was nothing worse than a friend beef. Emotions were known to fly out of hand, which eventually leads to innocent loved ones getting harmed. It was personal when you know a close individual who knew everything about you caused your entire life to fall.

"That's irrelevant. The same way I bleed, he bleeds. That bitch is not the hardest nigga walking around. If we take that li'l bread he toting, that'll calm all that arrogant shit down. He needs to lose, and once I got that bitch down bad, I'ma pop his ass with a whole clip." Reckless's finger twitched just from the discussion.

Sekoya entered the living room with her arms folded. "And what do you think will happen after you do that? It surely isn't gonna happen that way," she stated with a disturbed expression.

Reckless was lost for words because he didn't know how long she had been hiding out inside the crib. Standing to his feet, he flashed her an evil grin. "What are you talking about?"

"You know what the fuck I'm talking about, nigga. Y'all thinking that you gonna rob Ryan, and that's gonna go totally wrong in your behalf. Tyleema, what's wrong with you? That boy has helped you when you had nothing. How could you sit right here and plot on Ryan like that?" She flipped her attention to her friend.

Tyleema stuttered while fiddling with her hands. "Sekoya, just calm down. I can't help the way he feels. I'm just trying to find a better way to handle this. "

"It ain't this!" Sekoya yelled while rolling her neck. "This dumb-ass nigga right here got your mind fucked up. I can bet you one thing. It ain't about to happen, so whatever y'all two plotting about, you might as well flush it out of ya dumb-ass minds."

Reckless smirked before walking closer to her. "And what if I don't? Who's gonna make me stop. You?" He bit on his bottom lip as if he was waiting for her ass to say the wrong the thing.

Not backing down to his gangsta, she placed a hand on her hip. "Fuck nigga, you don't scare me. I don't care what you think Tyleema is doing for you. I'm not weak. I'm going to let Ryan know what you're up to. So ask him what he thinks about it when you see him pull up on you, nigga. "

Exhaling deeply, Reckless caved a hard right fist into her jaw. Stumbling backwards, Sekoya's head crashed against the edge of Tyleema's hard oak mini bar.

Standing over her motionless body, Reckless was breathing like a professional wrestler. "Bitch, I'm not the one. I told you!" he shouted.

Jumping to her feet. Tyleema ran to her side. "Oh my god. Reckless!" she cried loudly after viewing the thick blood that was leaking from her friend's head. She placed her shaky hand on Sekoya's chest. The dead pulse caused her to jump back. "You killed her, Reckless. You murdered my sister," she whispered as the salty tears began to drop down her face.

"Bitch, shut the fuck up!" He pulled his gun and placed it up to her face. "It was a fucking accident. You seen it." Reckless started to panic, looking back and forth from her to Sekoya's body.

"It wasn't a fucking accident!" Tyleema's face screwed up with anger. "Why didn't you just let her have it, Reckless? What the fuck am I gonna tell her mother?" she screamed.

Reckless's eyes grew wide. "Bitch, if you yell one more time, I'ma blow yo' shit all the way to Africa. Shut the fuck up, and get on your feet, now!" He lowered the barrel to the middle of her head.

Trembling in fear, she used the wall to help her stand. Her legs felt like noodles, and all she could do was stare at Sekoya, whose eyes glared up at the ceiling like in a horror movie. It was a day that she would never forget.

"I warned her about that slick-ass mouth. You know I wasn't trying to hurt her, right?" he asked with aggression in his tone. He pushed the gun into her jaw slowly.

She shook her head. It was obvious that Reckless had officially lost his mind, and the best thing for her scary ass to do was comply or either die. "Yes," she replied in a humble tone.

"Good. You know that I would never hurt you, but right now I need your help. We gotta hide her, and you're gonna help me. I understand this is your friend, but I'm gonna be the one who has to protect you. I know a prison sentence isn't what you want on your plate. That's twenty-five to thirty years max. It's your house, Tyleema. A house that you shared with her. You ain't got no choice," Reckless bribed her with his eloquent speech. Shit was real, and there wasn't no way he was about to lose his life to the chain gang for a bitch.

Tyleema wiped her tears away and clasped her hands together. "What the fuck are we supposed to do? I just can't leave her here, Reckless."

"We ain't gonna fucking leave her. We just gotta hide her. I'm not trying to scare you, li'l mama, but you gotta calm down and listen to me. I'm only seventeen. You're older, so act like it," he said calmly, putting the pistol back on his hip. He moved towards the kitchen and found a few large garbage bags sitting in top of the filthy counter top. Snatching them up quickly, he passed them off to her.

"You want me to put my fucking friend in a trash bag? This shit isn't right, Reckless. She deserves to be buried." Her facial expression was pleading for his mercy.

"Tyleema, I'm gonna be clear on where we stand. I fuck with you, but I won't hesitate to kill you. I said we're in this together. Put the trash bags over her body, and I'm gonna wrap her in a sheet," Reckless ordered with an evil look in his eyes.

Doing what she was told, Tyleema sniffled and could feel the tears about to pour again. Instead of bucking, she obliged and placed one giant bag over the top portion of Sekoya's body, repeating the same steps with her lower half. She looked up at Reckless.

"Get the sheet off the bed." He was pointing like she didn't know how the hell to get around her own house.

Tyleema still obeyed out of fear of being shot. All she wanted was her perfect chance to make her getaway from him, and then his ass would be grass. She opened the door to the first room at the edge of their hallway. She snatched the sheets off of the mattress.

Reckless stood at the door clutching the handle of his gun. "Hurry the fuck up!" he spat, putting a pep in her step.

She moved swiftly past him back to the living room. "You don't have to be pushy, man. You did this, not me." Tyleema unfolded the sheet and placed it over Sekoya's body.

"Bitch, shut the fuck up. She didn't like yo' ass anyway. All this hoe thought about was ways to please Ryan, Tyleema. The whole plan was to get the money, not fall in love," Reckless said while tying the sheet around her friend's dead body.

Tyleema knew that his words were true. The only thing that placed a crick in his statement was her friend's lifeless body that he was preparing to dispose of. The thought of Teona crossed her mind. It was surely going to be a tragedy when she found out about this. The closeness between her and Sekoya was undeniable. She just prayed that it was possible to make it out of her sticky situation alive.

After Reckless finished wrapping Sekoya tightly, he grabbed one side of her body. "Help me carry her up to the attic. Pick her up. "

Tyleema grabbed her feet, and lifted her lightly in the air. The dead weight was something serious, and you could smell the bowels Sekoya released on herself upon passing away. "Don't you think putting her up here is a bad idea? If you're trying to leave her, she will eventually start to stink, Reckless."

"Keep moving, bitch!"

They both carried her to the center of the home, and lowered her when they reached the hallway. Tyleema reached towards the ceiling for a thick clear string that led to the attic. She pulled it and released an old rusty metal ladder.

Reckless stared up into the dark roof and waved the heavy dust particles away from his vision. He turned to eye Tyleema. He shrugged. "I'll go up first. All you have to do is guide me up so I don't fall. "He picked Sekoya's body back up, and carried her slowly up the ladder.

The creaky metal shrilled like a set of hot wheels speeding off as he proceeded up one step at a time, eventually making his way to the top. He used his strength and pulled Sekoya up into the attic, dropping her body against the hardwood floor. A line of sweat dropped down his forehead. "Get up here. I still need your help." He eyed Tyleema as she stood on the ladder as if she wanted to make a run for it.

She climbed the last few steps and stood in the attic looking at his cold hearted face. "What else is it left to do?"

"You!" Reckless pulled his gun and fired one shot, hitting her between the eyes.

Her soul departed from her body before crashing against the hardwood floor next to her friend. Reckless watched her gasp for air. She eventually grew stiff and took her last breath.

Stepping over her, Reckless made his way back down the metal ladder. Upon reaching the bottom, he folded the steps back up and pushed the attic door closed. The loud noise erupting upon it closing sent a shiver through his spine. The entire thing was just an accident. He never intended to hurt Tyleema, but her weak emotions were making him paranoid. He wasn't about to take the sad way out by claiming an accidental murder, nor was he about to allow Tyleema to rat him out for a lesser plea.

He quickly cleaned the house of all the small things he touched. Reckless turned the A/C under 30 degrees and left out of the front door.

Chapter 6

Torey's spot, east side of Delaware
8:45 p.m.

Free watched as Torey locked the door behind their last few soldiers. The new trap that he started a few days back was a one night success. After putting the right people on game about the new product Ryan was toting, base heads were calling by the minute. The shit was so raw that Torey even got a call about an overdose a few hours back. You would think that alone would stop a junkie motherfucker from feeding their demons, but that shit was truly irrelevant. It made people crave it more.

Torey moved back over to the table and took his seat. From the look on Free's face, he could tell something was eating on his conscience. It was a habit that his sidekick carried with him since they first became tight. "What the hell's wrong with you, fool?" Torey asked.

Free inhaled on his cigarette harshly before smashing it out in the hardwood coffee table. "Your fucking people is the problem."

"What the fuck are you talking about, Free?"

"I'm talking about this nigga Ryan. This bitch come through here like he the king of the jungle. Eastside village ain't rocking with no north side rookies period. What the fuck makes him so special?" Free asked with a slight sound of hatred in his tone.

Torey knew that his friend was quick to dead anything or anyone that wasn't from their same struggle. If you didn't grow up in the same hood and suffer the same childhood, you were neglected, even if you were close like a father and son. It was designed to go down through the generations, and now it was his time to hear the east side speech.

Torey began to count a small stack of money and split the entire knot with Free, tossing him half of the dough on the table. He pointed with a stern finger. "That's why, Free, because he has something to offer. If it's something that you could benefit off, why would you want to mess that up?"

"'Cause my family didn't cherish paper, Torey, and neither did yours. We're takers; practically the entire Delaware is. That nigga came through this bitch with a smirk like we his puppets. He comes and drops off a few bricks for us to sell like we some poor cats. Why we just can't take it all?" Free spat before sitting back in his chair.

Torey gave him a blank look. "Nigga, that's my cousin. I don't play like that unless a motherfucker crosses me. Ryan always supported me back then, and he has yet to do anything to violate that respect. That makes him off limits."

Free huffed with a smirk. "You're running the east side hard, and been doing it for years. You ain't been needing him. That shit sounds weak."

Torey brushed the comment off and refused to let his young friend anger him with the vain speaking. Shit was known to get out of control with Torey when he overthought things. People could die, and all mercy for human life would escape his heart. After losing his mother and father at the age of one, he was placed into an orphanage and sent from group home to group home. His destination landed him in Delaware. That's where Ryan's auntie on his father's side adopted him as her own. It made him heartless, but warmed him that he actually had someone to call Mama. Eventually that love was token away also when she lost her life from a massive drug overdose. That day, his back turned against the world.

"Listen, Free. You gotta learn how to ease your mind, bro. I hate getting extra opinions about shit that I do because I'll lose control and think that everyone is playing with me. It's going good for us right now, and that's all that matters."

"I wouldn't give a fuck how much money he got, or what he can do. I don't trust him. Arrogance never lied, bro. We've had numerous snakes slide around us and claim to be the most truthful like they were the fucking messiah. What happened?" Free asked with a raised eyebrow.

Torey shook his head and fired up a rolled Garcia Vega. "That's the difference between me and you, Free. I don't mind killing someone who transgresses bounds, whether unknown, friends, or family. I have no heart for anyone. Not even you. That's the way that we gotta be, remember?" Torey said before walking off on him, heading for the back room. He pondered Free's statement about Ryan, and one thing was for sure: no one just gave anything away as a gift. It either came with a price or a life. If that turned out to be the cause within his journey with Ryan, he would cut ties before a fallout occurred. Torey's entire bloodline was nearly gone, and family was all he had in his corner for the second to survive. It was either hustle, or back to laying down the murder game. That would be a day that no one could escape. Once the beast was unleashed, there would be no compassion for anyone.

* * *

The next morning
Brooklyn, New York, Pink House Projects

The bright morning sky stretched across the horizon, and the new air was a blessing to Ryan's nostrils. The energy, even the people, had a different vibe in the Big Apple. There were only a few times before where he entered the fast streets of New York, but that was his younger days when Kimyetta was really organized with his father Raekwon. The cool and rich side of the tracks was nice until they finally reached the Brooklyn block.

Ryan looked over at Precious in the driver seat. "Are you sure we in the right spot?"

"I'm positive. I know you may be thinking about my uncle's reputation of being the man or whatever, but he is really low key, and he's not switching that for anyone. Not even my mama," she said, bringing the car to a halt in front of the apartments.

Ryan glanced around the area and noticed a large group of men who sported blue flags on their necks and heads. Their postures shifted when they spotted Precious's car park across the street from the property.

"Where the fuck are we?"

"We're at the Pink House projects."

"The Pink House projects? Your uncle stays in a Crip neighborhood?"

"Yes. It's one of the most dangerous hoods in Brooklyn, but safe enough to duck away from the world when you have enemies like my uncle. Let's go," she stated before opening the car door to step out.

Climbing out of the whip behind her, Ryan watched as the gang members slowly approached them. Their guns were visible, and Ryan counted at least twenty-seven men. Moving off his killer instincts, he pushed Precious behind him and reached for his pistol.

"Don't do that shit, cuz!" one of the men yelled before he closed the distance on Ryan. The man who stepped in front of him raised his hands to calm his hungry wolves down before speaking. "Wassup, li'l cuz? Never seen you around here before. Any reason you out here in the Pink spot?"

"I'm here for a family member, my nigga. We don't want any problems." Ryan grabbed Precious's hand to keep her close.

The man who stood face to face with him looked as if he wouldn't hurt a fly. His demeanor was extremely calm, but a distant lion could be seen in his pupils. He was obviously the head over the neighborhood. "Well, this ain't nothing but Crip shit round here, li'l one. I'm familiar with everybody out here. The name is Boo Daddy, and don't be confused, because the only thing that's sweet is my bullets. Turn around and leave."

"I'm here to see my uncle Lucci," Precious butted in with a slick tone.

"Lucci ain't got no family. At least none that I've ever heard of." Boo Daddy's tone was dismissive, and the men who stopped behind him moved as if they were ready to kill if he snapped a finger.

Ryan pondered on bucking, but that quickly subsided when he remembered that Precious wasn't toting a fucking gun. She was no street nigga, and she damn sure didn't know how to dodge a bullet for two people. His common sense began to sink in, and he lowered his tone. "Bro, all you have to do is tell Lucci that he got guests. He knew that we was coming up here, and I didn't take no ride to Brooklyn for nothing." Ryan looked him square in the eyes without budging.

Boo Daddy laughed. "You can't know who the fuck I am, fool? Straight from the west side of Savannah. 600 murda block." Boo Daddy was the man with a plan. His political ties in the world put puppy dog-ass niggas to shame. It was hard to get around a man who had his hands into everything. He was the one that gave back and raised up nothing but some brilliance. He was a lion when it came to the streets, because he gave respect in order to get it. Niggas would whisper that he was just an old Crip nigga, but his aura would show you that leadership was just a title. He was one of the ones who could actually walk the walk and talk the talk. There were no in-betweens, and his patience was known to run thin at any minute. "For your safety, I suggest you get the fuck out of here." He glared into Ryan's eyes, searching for any weakness.

Before Boo Daddy could order for Ryan to be removed, one of his li'l homies made his way hastily to the front of the crowd with a cell phone in hand. "It's Lucci."

Boo Daddy kept his eyes locked in on Ryan as he grabbed the phone and placed it up to his ear. "What's crackin'?"

"Let them in," Lucci's voice spoke calmly through the line.

Without responding, Boo Daddy ended the call and passed it back to his young henchmen. "I'ma be clear on one thing. This ain't no hood that you just can stroll up in, cuz. We real Crips, fool. Nothing touches this project unless I know about it. The next time, it'll be a fee. Just homage for the crew," he said with a straight face.

"I'll be sure to keep that in mind," Ryan said before stepping past them with Precious by his side.

The crowd of men stepped to the side, allowing them to pass. The disturbing faces he walked through didn't stop him from keeping eye contact until they reached the apartment building. Once they entered the main entrance, Ryan grabbed Precious by the shoulders and looked into her eyes. "Don't ever bring me somewhere like this if you know we have to go through some shit like this. They could've killed us." His face was showing signs of anger.

"I'm sorry, Ryan. I haven't been here in a while. I've never been through that any other time I've come see him, Ryan."

"When was the last time?"

Precious thought to herself. "I was about seventeen."

Slapping his forehead in disbelief, he shook the answer from his mind. "Let's just get this over with."

Precious nodded and led the way until they reached the second floor of the apartment complex. As they moved down the stinky and pissy hallway, Ryan covered his nose. The sight of the projects was worse than anything that he'd ever seen in Delaware. New

York was known to keep a building full of rats and a bunch of murderers who would kill for any unknown reason. There was no way a legend like Lucci Bruno would even fit into an atmosphere like the one he was experiencing at that second.

Precious stopped in front of door number 28 and looked back at Ryan. "This is it." She shrugged before knocking on the door three times.

The sound of a distant television could be heard inside. After a few seconds of waiting, the locks began to shuffle before the door opened up. The Italian man who stood in front of them flashed a small smile and wrapped Precious into a tight hug.

"Look how big you have gotten, princess. How are you?" He kissed both of her cheeks.

"I'm okay, Uncle Lucci. Your little friends outside just made us feel like we were being initiated into the ghetto league of criminals." She laughed.

"No worries, lovey. They're only doing what I asked, ya know? Too many people are talking, and I don't like a lot of whispers when it comes down to me." Lucci smoothed back his silky black hair before turning to Ryan. "You must be the lucky man who my princess tells me about?"

"I am," Ryan answered.

"It's a pleasure. The name's Lucci, kid. Come on in. I'll fix you two something to drink." He moved inside of the apartment.

Precious grabbed Ryan's hand and entered behind her uncle.

"So, I know you kids have been playing in Delaware for a while. How do you like the big city?" Lucci reached into his cabinet and grabbed two glasses.

Ryan couldn't help but to look around the medium-sized apartment. A sixty-inch plasma TV was mounted on the wall. Most of the furniture was hand-crafted cherry wood and leather from Italy. The aura of his home felt like the movie *Godfather*. Most of the portraits on the wall consisted of people like Al Pacino, Lucky Lucianno, and John Dillinger. You wouldn't expect to see such a nice crib beneath the walls of the Pink Projects.

"We love it. You know that my mom is being rebellious about me coming all the way up here to see you." Precious accepted the glass of milk that Lucci offered. Ryan declined his drink and took a seat on the couch next to her.

"Betty will always be Betty. She's my sister, and still treats me like I'm a child. Your mother is stern for a reason, Precious. Most of the time your father felt as if I would be a harm for your life. It caused my own flesh and blood to turn and treat me like I was a slave. I don't respect slave owners, princess. It's the reason I fight against oppression, especially when it comes to family. But on another note, what brings you and your friend to my domain?" Lucci said before taking a seat in his chair directly across from them.

"I wanna do business with you." Ryan leaned forward with his hands intertwined like a true business man.

"Why? You don't even know me."

"No disrespect, Lucci, but I think everybody knows who you are. You're a legend in Wilmington. Even my dad used to speak about you."

"And who is he?" Lucci replied sarcastically before sipping his glass of milk. He set down his cup and sparked a large cigar that rested on a small snack stand.

"His name's Raekwon. I don't think you know him personally, but you know how the word gets around," Ryan stated.

Precious placed the earbuds from her iPhone in to let their conversation proceed without her input. It was natural to let men handle business when it was something dealing with lots of money being on the line.

"You know, Ryan, I've heard millions of things spread from Italy to Chicago, New York to Wilmington, Florida to Jersey. Many men have things to spread, but the question is, what are they truly spreading? Could it be a lie? Maybe it's someone who wants attention. Or maybe it's someone who wants you to speak about matters that you have no knowledge of."

"I'm not understanding what you mean?" Ryan said with a curious face. The remark sounded like an insult, but he wasn't surprised, especially since he was dealing with an individual who was a one man army.

"It means that I can never trust a man who doesn't speak facts. People happen to spend a lot of time worrying about things that they have no knowledge of. Instead, I grew up finding out things to be able to learn more things. That's a box mind frame, kid. If your dad would have told you that I was the richest man in the world, would you have believed that?"

"Yeah, probably," Ryan answered.

"Exactly; because he's your dad. My dad told me that Christmas was real, and guess what happened when I found out the truth about Santa Claus?"

Ryan remained quiet, listening to the boss speak.

"I slashed him across the face with a razor. Placed a ten-inch gash, nearly cutting his tongue in two. That was because I refused to ever let a person lie to me again about something that I wanted to know." Lucci chuckled.

His dark black eyes told a painful story. Even from the way he was dressed, you could tell that his days of being a true don of the Italian Mafia were finally over. Lucci could stretch his hands through anybody's business, and all profits were a plus in his mind. It was the way of a true Italian. Live free. Die silent. Nothing more.

Ryan folded his arms with an arrogant smirk. "That's real. I would've probably did the same thing. But my dad is a real one. He would never lie to me for any reason, so I can't feel your pain on that one. I respect who you are whether we lie or tell the truth, but that's only if you're doing it for a good reason. "

"Respect can lean a mile and still have stumbles, son. You have to bump heads every now and then." Lucci placed his cigar stub on the metal snack tray. "So what's the gig? You didn't come this far with my niece to speak about life foundations."

"I got a proposition for you." Ryan kept eye contact, showing the hustler's ambition inside of him.

"I'm listening."

Ryan pulled an ounce of raw cocaine from his pocket and passed it to him. "That's just a sample of what I've touched. It's some of the purest dope pushing through Wilmington right now. I'm just not big on clientele. I know that if I get the right team of trusted buyers, we could make some good-ass money."

Lucci picked the drugs up and stared at the bag cautiously. He flipped out a switch blade, placed the point inside, and scooped up a small sample. Snorting a little, he lowered his head and rubbed the rest across his gums. He was quiet for about twenty seconds.

Ryan couldn't help but to say something. "So what do you think?"

Lucci cleared his throat and took a shot of the cold milk sitting in front of him. Sitting straight in his chair, he wiped his face before taking a deep breath. "Where did you get this from?

"I just told you, I'm from Delaware," Ryan said with a raised eyebrow.

"Ain't no one in Delaware connected on getting something like this. I'm everywhere, kid."

"You ain't right here." Ryan pointed down to the ounce of dope.

Lucci nodded. "You're absolutely right. I've been out of the game for a while, but I still dibble and dabble. What's the price?"

"Twenty-three for a key. If you buy more than fifteen, I can knock it down to an even twenty. I've flooded my hood in a matter of days, and I'm already being stalked for numbers that I'm not able to serve. I'm trying to get a higher supporter, if you see what I'm saying?" Ryan lied. He needed Lucci's help, and in order to keep any position the cartel had to offer, he needed a yes.

"You like my niece. I can tell by the way you look at her. We only have our balls and our word. Can you keep your word and be sure that she will never be involved in any of this? Business is business, but family is personal. If you support my niece in staying away,

I'll support you to make sure that the food is supplied for her." Lucci looked Ryan in the eyes with a serious-ass face.

"Done," Ryan replied, shaking his hand with a firm grip. "So is there any specific time you wanna do business?"

"Yeah. As soon as possible?"

Ryan couldn't help but to cheer on the inside. The thought of having Lucci Bruno on his side was impeccable. No one could reach a man of his caliber without paying your entire savings out. He was a mastermind. Not only was he a gangster, but his love for operating a drug business was like no other. He was the official missing link. "Cool. How many?"

"Twenty."

A wide smile began to spread across Ryan's face after hearing Lucci's number. After locking in his business deal, he set up a drop off for the same night and departed back to the car with Precious on his side. She couldn't help but to smile at him while they proceeded back down to the first floor of the apartment complex.

"What?" He blushed, glancing at her beautiful face. She was always happy for no reason.

"My uncle likes you. He doesn't have too many dealing with young teenagers when it comes to you guys' profession. That's a good sign. Were you satisfied with what his response?" she asked.

"Yeah, but I wanna ask you something. Why did you plug in your earbuds the entire time we were there?"

"Because. My uncle always told me that if I'm not listening, I wouldn't know anything if the cops ever approached me. That's the way I've been all my life. Why?"

"Nothing. That's understood." Ryan grinned.

The style of Lucci was like none other. Not only did he save Ryan a thousand more problems, but he gave advice that he held onto dearly.

Walking out of the New York complex, his mind thought about how DJ would feel about the overnight accomplishment. The plan was to get rich, and that's exactly what was about to happen.

Chapter 7

Ryan's house, Northside Philadelphia
10:45 p.m.

Ryan moved around the living room of his crib furiously. He was calling Sekoya's shit like a hotline. After twenty-six times in the last three hours, he still hadn't received an answer. It took him almost sixteen hours to get the right things in order, but she had his last five keys of cocaine in her possession. None of her slimy little friends could be reached, and the meeting with Richard was less than an hour away.

DJ sat on the sofa glancing at his cell phone. "She's probably having trouble getting that shit off, Ryan. I'm guessing she's probably scared to answer the call. You ain't heard from her since Friday. Today is Sunday."

"DJ, now is not the time for keeping shit real. We got a time limit. I'm trying to think positive, but now you making me feel like I need to find this girl and kill her." Ryan pulled out his pistol and reached for the car keys on his counter.

DJ grabbed ahold of his shoulders to calm him down. "Ryan, you have to chill, bro. If you panic right now, you'll blow everything."

"No one can know about this. Don't you understand that? What if she says something to somebody? The cartel is a secret, DJ. If they find out I'm dealing with any of you, I'm dead."

"I'm listening to you, but how can she say anything about the table when she doesn't know, Ryan? She's only a worker. Dig in your stash for the missing money, and replace it when you get the extra from Sekoya. It's only to clear your face. You got this."

Ryan exhaled before rubbing his chin. "You're right. I got this. If that trick ain't back with my dough by tomorrow though, I'm pulling up on all them bitches."

"I agree." DJ shrugged.

Ryan nodded and headed straight for his stash spot. Upon entering his room, he pushed his dresser off the wall and entered the code in his steel safe. There wasn't much saved up, but it was enough for him to cross the border and invest. That was the entire plan. To save, and not spend. Once his second meet up went accordingly, he would take the game by the throat until it crumbled.

Grabbing the necessary cash, Ryan stuffed it inside his duffle. It was gonna take his entire stash in order to cover the missing product, so Sekoya was on a thin line for the past due payments. After readjusting the dresser, he headed back for the living area, where DJ stood patiently. "I'll be back within two hours."

"I'll still be here, bro. Just be easy. Handle this business, and we will knock the rest of this out later." DJ patted his shoulder.

"We ain't got no other choice." Ryan dapped his man up before leaving his apartment. Looking down at his watch, which read 11:05, he prepared himself to see the boss. Within two weeks, he'd pushed more dope through Wilmington than any nigga on the entire north side. His deadline was near, but the necessary tools from Precious showed up to grant him the successful keys. After this next re-up, he was shooting for the entire state of Delaware.

* * *

Wilmington, Delaware.
45 minutes later
Randy's Sport's Bar

After pulling inside the establishment's parking lot, Ryan fixed his collar to his thick leather coat. He moved to the trunk of his car, removed his small duffle bag, and tossed it across his shoulder. After removing another large bag, he closed the trunk and headed for the entrance. The same two bodyguards were posted, but this time both men parted, allowing him to enter with no question.

Upon stepping inside, he paused, looking at the small crowd inside. The scenery was the same as the first time, and he could tell that the citizens weren't aware of what was transpiring underneath their feet. He walked over to the bar.

Lizzy spotted his face and smiled. "Well how are you, honey bun?"

"I'm good. Will this be the same process as last time?" Ryan shifted his eyes to the bags in his hands.

"You can head on down, sweet puff. You don't need me," she whispered with a straight face.

Nodding, he pushed towards the back and entered the door that led him to the basement floor, closing it behind him. He headed down the stairs and found himself walking up to the locked steel door just as he had the first time. After knocking three hard times, he set the bags down and pulled out his membership card. The hard latches sounded off once they were opened, and another large bodyguard stepped out with a disturbing face.

"Card?" His voice was thick and lethal.

Ryan smirked and passed him the ignition ticket. He watched the bodyguard look back up into his eyes. He placed the card back into Ryan's palm and moved to the side for him to enter.

Picking up the bags, he trailed inside and slowly made his way around the corner, where the entire table sat awaiting his presence.

Richard was the first to smile and stand. "Ryan, it's a pleasure to see you. I thought that you would be running late. We don't tolerate that, so it's great to see that you've made the time limit. Let me take this off your hands." He grabbed the bags from Ryan's hand and passed them off to Summer and Winter, the two redheaded assassins.

Without replying to Richard's comment, Ryan watched as all the eyes followed him until he took his seat. No one spoke or made a sound until the clock touched twelve midnight.

Richard glanced at his watch and placed his hands together. "I thank you all for coming tonight. I'm hoping that we've had a great week. I've been hearing things in the streets. Movements, sales, it's all a part of the way we eat. We control a small number of uptown States, but lacking will place us in the dirt. I mean, I don't know about you guys, but I would kill the idiot who tarnishes the name of a table that I'm eating at. We all know a bullet to the brain eases the body." Richard laughed loudly.

Everyone continued to remain silent. The indirect threat was clearly for the entire table.

"But that's on another note." Richard smoothed the side of his curly hair. "Are there any unsuccessful deals, or problems I need to know about from anybody?"

The room was still dead silent. Ryan spotted Detective Bradley appearing from that spooky-ass back office. He held a small piece of paper in his hand. He passed it to Richard. Bradley winked at Ryan and then disappeared back to his destination, the little-ass back room.

Richard scanned the paper as if he was reading a ransom note for his daughter. It didn't take longer than thirty seconds before he placed the paper face down. "Well, it seems like we only have one problem, and it's with you, Ryan." Richard's head turned to him in a fast motion. "You added up for your entire supply. Have you been working with someone?"

Ryan was caught off guard by his question, but held shit down like a real one. "I don't work with nobody but myself. I did what I was supposed to do. "

"That's absolutely correct. You did what you were supposed to. I'm just wondering, how did you do it?"

Richard's face was still searching for a direct answer. The other ten members of the table sat around with unreadable expressions.

Shit became weird for Ryan within those few seconds. The hittas, Summer and Winter, stood behind Richard with small grins of evil tracing their lips. His tongue shuffled up, but he remembered everything that was counting on this one shot. He couldn't fuck it up.

"I can't help it that I can stretch my wings and deal with my people. No one is grounded with my business. I'm alone. Operations are run through me only. I'm a businessman. Money has to be made," he said, waiting for a bullet to fire at any second. Ryan had already witnessed motherfuckers get executed right in front of him. There was nowhere to run because one of the members would probably gun you down before you could hurt anyone.

Richard stood to his feet and clapped loudly. "Brilliant young individual. This is the reason we've raised the children to be smarter than us. Ryan is younger than most of you, and he's mastered the key to our table. He said that he's a businessman who has to make the money alone. Ryan, the reason I ask this is because the limit for everyone at this table is twenty every two weeks. You've sold forty, which is a double. No one has ever done it since I've been running this operation. So I'll ask again. Have you spoken to anyone outside of the board about the business? Delaware isn't able to push forty keys within two weeks."

Ryan couldn't believe his ears. All members were looking at him suspiciously. It was probably the same reason Richard was questioning him about his dealings with the people. "I said no. I've put in my own work before I started sitting at this table. I learned how to follow simple instructions in school. Nobody knows about the table, and that's the only thing that matters." Ryan sat back with a calm posture as Richard stared him down.

Breaking the silence with a smile, he shot Ryan a thumbs up. "This is great news that Ryan has brought to us. Of course, we know the rules. Everyone at the board is equal, which means if Ryan is selling forty a week, you guys' shipment will be rising to the same number as him. I've never seen a rookie to the table accomplish more than a vet. Take this opportunity to speak now if any one of you isn't going to be able to handle the new contract. Speak now or forever hold your peace."

No one in the room offered a syllable. All their eyes continued to beam on Ryan for some odd apparent reason. The hating didn't matter to him. A motherfucker couldn't get mad because he had the gift to handle the business sufficiently in a small amount of time. The few men who sat at the table were obviously nonprofessionals because Ryan didn't know a damn thing about the game.

Richard glanced at his time piece and decided to end the meeting until the next two week session. "Listen, you guys. Lizzy should have a package for most of you upstairs. If not, then you'll be extended an extra day and have to do a pick up tomorrow. Good evening, Cartel." He lightly bowed his head and entered the small room with Winter and Summer behind him.

Ryan raised up from the table with a smile. Of course he wanted to be the first back upstairs to get near Lizzy, a job he had successfully proven he could handle shit with no pressure.

As they all made their way back to the top floor, a few whispers came from a couple of the members of the table. Of course it was out of earshot, so Ryan couldn't hear the secret conversation that was going on about him.

When Ryan reached the counter, he tapped lightly to get Lizzy's attention.

"Hey honey bun, are you ready for me?" she asked, reaching for one of the giant trash bags behind her. It took her a second to pass it over the counter, but Ryan was able to grab ahold of it with a firm grip.

Lizzy flashed a smile. "Hopefully I'll see you leave this alone soon," she whispered. "My son is around your age, and I've only seen one man who was good enough to keep this going. Save and quit, because it only ends one way with these people," Lizzy warned with a fake smile before turning to finish her duties.

"Okayyy. Weird-ass lady," Ryan mumbled before heading for the front entrance and then making his way slowly to the car.

She placed the re-up in his trunk and slammed it close. When Ryan turned around, he faced a tall black man with a low haircut. His waves were spinning in a 360 and his tailored suit made him appear to be a car salesman. He was clearly one of the table members because his face was memorable. He was the arrogant bastard from Atlanta, the nigga who spoke with assurance about his business. It was weird because he had never spoken to Ryan before.

"Wassup? Can I help you?" Ryan asked with a suspicious mug?

"Yeah, I just wanna know, why did you unbalance the table? Are you aware of what just occurred?"

"What? I don't know what the fuck you're talking about, buddy. If you were down there with me, then we are obviously on the same page," Ryan stated with a hint of aggression.

"You just caused all of us to be put on a timer. We've sold twenty kilos every two weeks for the past year and a half. You've come along, done whatever magic trick you thought of, and it's caused us to go under with you." Simion folded his arms.

"I'm not going under shit, my dude. You don't even know me, and for the record, fuck the table. I work for myself!" Ryan spat before getting in his Infiniti truck.

Ryan dismissed the true shit that the stranger was trying to tell him. Ryan was sure to smash out of the driveway with his tires screeching. Mission accomplished. Now shit was about to switch. It was time for a payday, one that would make all the same bitch-ass niggas who hated him bow at his feet.

Chris Green

Chapter 8

The sound of loud knocking could be heard on Ryan's front door. It caused him to jump up from his sleep and grab his Glock .357 handgun from underneath his pillow. Stepping out of his bedroom door, he watched as DJ peeped though the small hole to see who was on the other side. Looking back at Ryan, he waved his hand to calm his nerves.

DJ opened the front door, letting Teona walk inside. Her face was drenched in tears, and she looked l as if her entire world was destroyed. As she walked over to Ryan, she shook lightly. "Ryan, what happened?"

Ryan wiped his face as if he was exhausted. "Teona, it's six-thirty in the morning. Why are you banging on my fucking door like the police, and what the hell are you talking about?

"Sekoya's dead," she cried lightly. "What in the fuck is going on?"

"What!" Ryan's eyes grew wide before looking over to DJ to see if he heard the same thing escape her mouth. "What do you mean Sekoya's dead? That's impossible. "

"Ryan, they found her in the attic of her house wrapped in sheets. Tyleema's dead too. She was shot in the head. "

"No fucking way." DJ began to pace around in a panic.

Ryan was still stuck in disbelief. The shocking news took him by surprise, and he honestly didn't know what to say. The thought of Sekoya and Tyleema dead made him wonder who was next. If someone was doing this for a purpose, they damn sure made an example, and Ryan wasn't about to sit around and wait for it to come. "First of all, we gotta take a deep breath, and find out what the fuck is going on. Who the hell would want to hurt Sekoya and Tyleema?

"I don't know, Ryan. That's why I'm here." Teona wiped her puffy eyes.

"This is some sick shit. These bitches just end up dead after we've all been kicking it around them for the past month? That ain't strange?"

Pondering DJ's remark, Ryan lightly grabbed Teona's shoulders. "When is the last time you seen Sekoya?"

"Probably about two days ago. They were fine before I left the house. Sekoya was supposed to go and take care of some business, and Tyleema was waiting for...Reckless." Her eyes began to pour once again. "Oh my God. I think Reckless did this."

"Wait, you just can't say that," DJ tried to defend him.

"He was the only one able to get near them. Tyleema was following him around like a sick puppy. Sekoya didn't like the fact that he was speaking badly about Ryan, and she warned Tyleema to start backing away from him."

"That doesn't mean that he killed them, Teona. We can't just blame him." DJ shook his head with a disbelieving expression. "Maybe it was someone they did bad business with. We don't know."

"DJ, she's right." Ryan snapped out of his trance.

"You're saying that, bro, but how do you know?"

"Because Sekoya is a rock alone type chick. She doesn't deal with anyone. For the past two weeks, she was filling me in on the bullshit that he was kicking about us. Reckless didn't want Sekoya to rock with me because he wasn't a part of our movement. We haven't seen this nigga since the hospital incident. That bitch pulled a slick stunt, and now he hiding out," Ryan guessed. It was common sense to him. No one inside of Delaware had the nuts to try them. It wasn't a coincidence that Sekoya and Tyleema became a casualty of Ryan's game. It was always the things that you didn't see, and at that time, it was Reckless.

"What the hell are we gonna do, Ryan? You started this shit. Tell me what the fuck to do!" Teona yelled in pain.

Ryan grabbed her by the shoulders, shaking her lightly. "Teona, shut the fuck up. I'm going to handle this shit, but you gotta calm the fuck down. I can't think if you're yelling and panicking. Do you understand?"

Snapping out of her hurt aura, she nodded in compliance.

Ryan looked over to DJ. "Bro, we're gonna pull up and find out what the fuck is going on. We pulling up on this nigga, and if his story doesn't add up, I'm killing his stupid ass."

"Ryan, you know if we slide up on Reckless he's gonna spazz out. It's like you asking for something to happen. Just call him, and have a talk," DJ suggested.

"He ain't trying to talk, nigga. Sekoya's fucking dead. All we have to do is pull up. If he act stupid, then you should know that something is up. Teona, you need to just go to the nearest gas station from the block and wait for our call. If we don't find out what's going on right now, it'll be too late when whoever the fuck did this comes for us."

DJ nodded, and placed both hands over his face for a few seconds. "You right. All we need to do is try and talk. He shouldn't have no reason to act out," he tried to convince himself. The team had been out of whack for a while, and it was obvious that everybody's feelings were deeply involved some kind of way. It was eight and a half months before DJ left for Princeton University, and he wasn't trying to miss it for a murder case playing around with Reckless.

Ryan headed to the room and placed on a fresh set of clothes. He grabbed his Glock .357 handgun and checked the clip before placing it on his hip. It was messed up what happened to Sekoya and Tyleema. That threat was a serious message, but it wasn't about to take long for a reply. If Reckless caused death upon those girls, he was now gonna have to add Ryan to that list.

Chapter 9

Faith's house, 10:34 a.m.

The sun was shining brightly through Faith's window as she moved around her living room cleaning. Ryan had promised to stop by on that day to pick up Prince for a day out. The hours were already passing, and she automatically began to doubt his promise.

After walking over to Prince, she lifted him out of his car seat and took a seat on the couch. Grabbing the small baby bottle of Similac, she placed it into his mouth. The thought of her catastrophe with Ryan was bugging her lately. There was a point in time where he wouldn't let her out of his sight. Ever since he decided to get into the game heavy, his heart was becoming black. Ms. Anderson was even able to spot his new arrogant swagger. She said that the money was only a way to hide his pain. He couldn't be a father and a true provider because he didn't know how to. Her mother's words were beyond true. Ryan had been her high school sweetheart, the one that she felt would last for eternity. Now that Prince had come into the world, his feelings left.

The sharp knock at her door broke the small daydream that held her. After setting little Prince back in his seat, she headed for the door, thinking that Ryan had finally come through for a change. After seeing Demerea through the peephole, she huffed and opened the door.

"Hey bitch." She smiled before walking in all ghetto and shit.

"Hey Demerea. What are you doing here? I thought you was planning your trip to New York for work?"

Demerea sat on the couch and pulled a rolled blunt from her Gucci tote. "I was, but I don't know if I wanna leave without throwing me a leaving party. I gotta build myself up before I move away to another city. "

"Ain't that the truth? I'm trying to feed this big-ass baby. He getting big already." Faith sat back next to his car seat.

"I can tell. He looks just like Ryan."

Hearing his name, Faith balled up her face. "Please, bitch, don't remind me. I'm starting to puke."

Demerea laughed and smacked her lips. "Hoe, you know Ryan got your pussy in a titanium safe. He branded yo' ass."

"Ryan ain't branded shit. That nigga barely making it by with the slick shit he already doing. I'm two seconds away from dismissing his ass and showing him that child support and a new man could happen overnight."

"When are y'all gonna work on getting back together?" Demerea asked with a raised eyebrow.

"What do you mean get back together?" Faith's heart paused for a second.

Demerea looked at Faith as if she was late on the dirty news. It was obvious that Ryan had ditched her, but no one even had the heart to tell her about the deceit. That was officially about to end. "Faith, you know that you're my friend first off. I love you like a baby sister, but that man has a grown bitch. She got my money. She pretty as fuck, and them folks building shit together, that club a few miles out. The Royal. That's their shit. I found that out through a few of my associates," she admitted.

"What? How do you know this? What girl?" Faith was about to instantly have a meltdown. She had never caught Ryan in the act of cheating, but always had her suspicions. Now it was even deeper when a dear friend was telling her about some shit that she wasn't even aware of.

"Her name is Precious. A little cute-ass red chick with long hair. Fake-ass Lauren London-looking hoe, but she only wish that she can play NeNe from ATL." Demerea tried to add a small joke to break her tension.

Faith sat in silence for a moment before replying. "So my family is really over?" she asked out loud.

Huffing, Demerea put out her lit blunt. "Girl, you better wake the fuck up. You are young and fine. Do you know how many niggas out there looking for a good girl? What he don't love is what he'll miss. Your family is just beginning. You just have some adjustments to do. Take my advice for once. That man ain't good for you, Faith. Usually I don't say anything, but I can't keep letting this go. He's moved on. It's time to just face the truth. "

Faith stared at her baby boy and dropped a small tear from her left eye. "Wow, I've had a child and lost the love of my life within days. Maybe this wasn't a good idea, Demerea." She started to slowly break down harder.

"No, bitch. Ryan wasn't a good idea. You should have been snapped out of that fake-ass snooze and been searching for some side meat, because that bastard ain't never about to change. Men are men, Faith.

It's only one way with them. He doesn't love you obviously. "

Faith folded her arms in submission. "I'm guessing that it just wouldn't hit me. I never thought Ryan would leave me. I gave him a son. Maybe I just need to call him and work out this misunderstanding." She reached for her cell phone on the glass table.

"No!" Demerea quickly snatched her line. "Did you not hear what I just told you? That boy has another girl. I seen her with my own eyes. If you tell him, he's gonna know that I told you, Faith. I don't want to be in the middle. There ain't nothing that you can do about it but move on, girl. "

Nodding, Faith rocked her foot in anger. "I'll make him wish that he never played with me. I don't really have it all, but I had patience. He just thinks leaving me about to be sweet, but I bet you that I can show him different," Faith promised.

Smirking, Demerea rolled her eyes. "Sure, you can always do that, but first think about what's best for your child. If it's gonna cause more pain, you should probably just consider to let it be."

"Whatever." Faith ignored her friend's plea. No man was able to conquer her heart like Ryan did. There was no such thing as living a life without him. Faith's mind pondered on a few evil thoughts. The pain Ryan was causing hurt dearly, like a poisonous spider draining its venom through the center of her veins. The feeling was surreal. Honesty only dug her a grave, and a lie would push her in a full circle. Demerea was right; she had no win. The fake love that she shared with Ryan was used like a gas station pump serving a hundred customers. It was all in vain. It was safe to say that those who sometimes had trust in you would go astray. Even if you strived to make them happy. That moment of her life was over. From that day forward, there was only one way: a closed heart, and a new demeanor that would show you just how crazy shit could get.

* * *

Ryan had been riding around in his car with DJ for the past three hours. They had stopped by numerous locations that Reckless was known to crash at on the regular. No one would make a peep as to whether or not they had viewed his slimy ass moving through the hood, so Ryan knew that there was a little foul play in the air.

"Maybe he just laying low somewhere until Wicked comes home. You know this nigga be all depressed and shit." DJ was trying to think positive instead of dirty. Shit that the tongue would speak on had a funny way of prevailing if you put a little too much conversation to it.

"Nah, he ain't."

"How do you know, bro? You been with me for the past four days." DJ gave him a pathetic look.

"Because he's right there." Ryan pointed to him posting on the block in front of the small liquor store. His mind was so wrapped in a discussion with a young female that he never saw the Infiniti truck pull up directly behind him.

Just from the look in shorty's eyes, Reckless could sense her posture stiffen and change before she asked the magic question. "Who are those guys?"

Turning around to see Ryan and DJ walking towards him, Reckless wasted no time pulling his gun and letting off three slugs.

Ryan and DJ quickly scrambled, ducking for cover. The young woman screamed and dropped down to the ground out of fear of being shot.

After finding safety behind his truck, Ryan looked at DJ with an angry expression. "Does that shit answer yo' question, dummy?"

DJ couldn't help but to duck his head as Reckless fired three more loud shots. "Okay, well, I guess he's hiding something."

"You think?" Ryan yelled before leaning around the car, aiming his Glock .357. It roared louder than a train. Boom! Boom! Boom! Boom! Boom!

"I don't know what y'all niggas thought, but you'll die before I lay down, pussy!" Reckless yelled before firing his good again and jolting for the alleyway by the raggedy liquor building.

Stepping out to release another shot, Ryan watched the back of Reckless's feet disappearing behind the establishment like lightning. "Fuck!" he raged before jumping back in the car to chase him down.

DJ moved hastily to climb back in the passenger seat to stop him. "Ryan, we have to go. If you try and follow him, the entire department of Delaware police will be on our ass before we get past the third red light. Let's go home now." His face showed no type of emotion, and Ryan could feel his energy.

"Motherfucker!" Ryan slammed his fist on the steering wheel and smashed off the opposite way.

After passing through the next couple of intersections, DJ looked behind them and took a deep breath.

"We're going to find him, bro. We just have to think. You're a businessman now. If you stop, everything will end."

Ryan knew that his brother's words was true. The new shipment that was sitting in his bedroom caused him to rethink the nasty thought of killing Reckless while the sun was still smiling and shining. "I told you, DJ. We can't trust these niggas. He's definitely guilty, and that weak-ass stunt he just pulled proved it."

"You're right. Now we need to handle this shit quietly as possible. You must forgot that the entire Newark High knows about you and Reckless's fallout. You don't need the drama, bro. Wait until the time is right," DJ plotted with a sad look. It was crazy that it had to be so sectioned off between friends who had come from the dirt together. It was bound to expose itself, and today happened to be that day. Regardless of how DJ felt, Reckless's actions were beyond the limit of beef. Shit was real, and there was guaranteed to be a nasty retaliation. Ryan was rocking shit to sleep, and DJ knew that he was gonna catch that boy slipping and burn his ass like a bowl of diseases. That was a day that he just wasn't prepared for.

"My mind is made up. He's dead when I catch him," Ryan stated clearly.

"What about Wicked?"

"If he knows what's good for him, he's going to stay in his lane and accept that his cousin was a pest."

"Ryan, Wicked just got a year in prison for that armed robbery yesterday. He called me from the wall phone. I didn't want to tell you because it was already enough sitting on your table. You don't want him to come home knowing that you murdered his cousin, bro. He's gonna react back, without a doubt," DJ warned.

"What! That nigga just shot at us and you sitting here like we gotta spare him because Wicked is a friend? Well, think again, nigga, 'cause I'm slumping that bitch!" he spat with venom flying from his tongue.

"Ryan, I only speak because I care, dog. All I'm saying is play smart. It's easy ways to get rid of a nigga without getting ya hands dirty. You got the money to make it easy."

Ryan was about to reply, but froze when the unmarked police cruiser behind them flashed their sirens. "Shit!" Grabbing his pistol, he quickly tucked it in his waistband.

DJ glanced in the rearview and could see the Crown Victoria speeding up. "What you gonna do, bro. If we run, this shit is gonna make the news. Maybe it's just a routine traffic stop."

Ryan wanted to mash the gas pedal, but something told his conscience not to. He slowed the vehicle down. He pulled over and stopped the Infinti truck completely. "If they say anything dumb, I'm mashing the gas with no remorse."

"It is what it is," DJ replied.

Two officers stepped out of the vehicle. They proceeded to both sides of Ryan's truck. Once the officer on his driver's side got closer, he realized that it was none other than Detective Bradley. "Just be cool. It's Bradley," Ryan whispered before his police ass tapped on the glass window with two knuckles.

Ryan eased both front windows down with the click of a button. "Is there a problem, officers?"

Detective Bradley lowered his head and looked at Ryan with a weird grin. "Good evening, Mr. White. Can I see your license and registration please?"

Ryan was so distraught that he didn't notice Detective Furlow from the hospital standing on DJ's side of the car. Instead of showing any signs of anger, he reached for the info that was stuffed inside of his sun visor. "Here you go, my dude. That's everything." Ryan slapped the papers into his hand.

"Watch yourself, boy. You must be overheated in this fake-ass Mercedes." Bradley cocked his head to the side.

"I think he is," Furlow added.

"No sir. No problem. We just wanna be on our way." Ryan killed the negative energy quick.

"Step out of the car, sir?" Detective Bradley smiled.

"What?"

Jacking the door open, he snatched Ryan out and pushed him against the car.

"Man, what the fuck are you doing? Get the fuck off me!"

Detective Furlow followed the same routine with DJ, placing them both into handcuffs.

Detective Bradley whispered in Ryan's ear, "You riding around this bitch like you supposed to have friends, motherfucker."

"I ain't doing shit, nigga. You need to take ya greasy-ass cuffs off me. You know what the fuck going on," Ryan mumbled as he watched Detective Furlow scan the front seats for anything illegal.

Patting him down, Detective Bradley felt the handle of a gun on his waist. Lifting Ryan's shirt, his face glowed in excitement. "You talking hard like you ain't got a whole ten year bid on your hip, boy. How we supposed to do this? I bet Richard would be highly upset if you fumble your mission and end up behind bars today." Detective Bradley was sure to watch his tone so his new partner wouldn't intrude.

"Why would you do that when you would be the reason I'm going to jail, Bradley? Just let me get back in the car and leave."

Ryan was trying to study Detective Bradley's face to figure out what was about to be said next. The quick slip would be drastic, but he would definitely have to address Richard on what was going on. Ryan could tell by his silence that he didn't want any trouble.

Detective Bradley lowered Ryan's shirt to cover the gun handle. "If you think that you're gonna be in my city doing what the fuck you want to, think again. I have a job to do, Royal, and it ain't about to slow up for you. You either ride alone, or don't ride at all. I'm all around this bitch, and if you make me book you, then we will just see how that ends for you. Act like you getting money," Bradley spoke in a low tone.

"Cuffs." Ryan ignored his statement and shook his wrists with irritation.

"What did you find over there, Furlow?" Detective Bradley yelled, never taking his eyes off Ryan.

"I don't see nothing." He stood out of the vehicle and removed the plastic gloves on his hands. "Suspect is also clean."

Ryan mugged Bradley after he placed a hard slap on his shoulder. The little show he just put on was epic, but it surely wasn't about to become a habit. That was something Ryan would break in a quick matter of time.

Bradley released the cuffs on his wrist. "I guess you got lucky this time, Mr. Delaware. One slip, and yo' ass will be grass. Remember that shit." He pointed his finger lightly towards Ryan's chest. "Furlow! It's time to let these gentlemen go on about their way. Something telling me that one of 'em got somewhere to be." He smirked before flashing a crooked-ass smile.

Detective Furlow released DJ from the handcuffs and allowed him to get back in the car. The two officers stared them down until they closed the truck doors and pulled off.

DJ had a line of sweat dripping down his head. The thought of jail wasn't anywhere in the category of his mind at the time. By the grace of God, it fell accordingly. After making the next right turn to exit the main street, Ryan's facial expression loosened up.

"That nigga is a pest. He wanna be seen, and I don't know how long I'ma let his little stunts slide. That was his first and last time trying me," Ryan stated calmly as if nothing just happened.

DJ stared at him with wide eyes. "That nigga didn't feel that big-ass gun on yo' hip?"

Ryan smiled. "Of course he did. I'm just a factor, so it's nothing he can truly do about it. If you remove me, you take money from your own plate. He needs me."

"That's some deep shit, Ryan. That dude isn't good business." DJ glanced behind them once more to make sure they were in the clear.

"I'm not worried about him period. Right now he doesn't hold any weight. You see what just occurred back there? We got a golden ticket. Niggas ain't getting let go when they got a burner in the car. I gotta be doing something right." Ryan shrugged. "If anything, we need to be worried about this dirty-ass fool Reckless, 'cause it's about to get real ugly with him. Just relax, because I'm gonna handle everything."

Instead of replying back, DJ gazed out of the passenger side window. The thought of all that he possessed flashed through his. If his mom only knew that he was placing his scholarship at risk for a wild-ass homeboy... Regardless of how long he wasted in the streets of Wilmington, he achieved a pass to one of the best schools where the other people said Blacks couldn't go. Not only was his life paved, it was laced with a little red carpet and pampering. DJ's mom and dad was extremely big on working hard for what you dreamed to see. Their bank accounts alone could lace him, and their next three generations, if the bright seed could manage. All he had to do was walk through the damn door.

Ryan tapped his shoulder. "You alright, nigga? Snap out of that shit. We gotta stay focused. This shit ain't about to move itself. Reckless has crossed that bridge for the last time, so my mind is set on that. All we need to do is make this money, and set you straight before you leave for Jersey."

He couldn't say anything at the second, so he just smiled to mask away those evil tragedies of defeat. No one was going to determine his life, but the extra money for his classes and utensils was gonna be needed. Ma Dukes and Pop surely weren't an option because they knew that DJ was self-sufficient. He was always capable of handling shit on his own. It was the reason he was able to shine bright over a lot of others. He just prayed that his vision wasn't shattered for some shit that wasn't meant.

"I can guarantee you this, DJ. If you ride with me, and we tighten up the loose screws of our ship, we will leave this shit with all the money we can see. You gotta just trust me. I know what I'm doing," Ryan boasted like drug dealing was a real profession.

"I hear you, Ryan," DJ replied. He was listening, but his attention was clearly elsewhere. All he could think about was not failing. Not even for Ryan.

Chris Green

Chapter 10

Wilmington detention facility
4:30 p.m., maximum security pod

Standing out of his metal bunk, Cheek Raw grabbed his large bathing towel and soap dish from his box. The loud buzzing door was still clinking like an old Chevy motor, and you could tell that the prison was slowly falling apart. Kicking the door lightly, it opened wide enough for him to slide his body through. The maximum security dorm was always twenty-three hours lockdown and one hour a day for every individual inmate. All your ass could do was shower and stare at the same old-ass movies on the small Panasonic television.

The cold-ass day room was empty, and all the lights were dim for the two hour quiet time. After walking down the flight of steps, he entered the large walk-in shower section. He set his fresh clothes on the wall, stepped out of his boxers, and turned on the shower head. The steam instantly began to fill up the room.

Just as he started to bathe, hairs on the back of his neck began to rise. Turning around, he saw four men strapped with two homemade knives apiece standing less than ten feet away from him. Their demeanor was calm, and the biggest of the men slowly stepped forward when he realized their presence was known.

"You know what it is, Cheek."

Realizing he was caught down bad without his shank, Cheek wiped the light water from his face.

"What the fuck is this about? I don't mind cutting bread, my nigga." His heart was pounding harder than six car speakers.

The other three men began to close in slowly as the leader continued to speak. "Word is you food, bitch. They got a hundred stacks on yo' head, and I need that tab, Cheek."

"I ain't no pussy, Rico. I been in Delaware my entire life. I can double that shit, bro. I'll give you two hundred. Wherever you want it sent, my nigga." Cheek used his hands to cover himself. The sharp rusty metal was bound to shred him to pieces if he ran to the control booth for help, and four men was already a loss awaiting.

Rico stared him in the eyes and whipped out a slim piece of metal that resembled a machete. "Your money is dead, nigga. I've already been paid."

"Come on, bro, we ain't gotta rock like this," Cheek pleaded. He moved sideways as the men surrounded him.

Rico made the first move by swinging the blade towards his face. Cheek dodged the vicious attack by an inch. Before he could try to defend himself, one of the inmates slammed a blade into the back of his head.

All he could muster was a light grunt before falling to the ground to do what a scary nigga without a gun does best. Ball up. By the time he touched the ground, all four men gang piled him and released their blades, swinging unmercifully. His face was being hit, and a thick gash spread across his face with every hit Rico delivered. The other three men continually stabbed him in the back and chest until he passed out from the heavy trauma. That still didn't stop the ruthless inmates from kicking his face into submission. By the time they were all done, Cheek laid in a pool of blood with a disfigured face. Every breath he took caused his chest to lightly jump. The sight of the inmates lifting him inside a rolling laundry cart forced his heart to slow down more.

After throwing him inside, Rico looked down into his eyes. He was losing so much blood that he couldn't even muster a word. Rico raised his hand and slammed the knife once more across his forehead. The loud thud instantly placed him to sleep, and a thin trail of blood began to slide down his nose. Within seconds, he was folded in a fetal position inside the small bin and took his last breath. His bowels could be smelled after two of the killers began piling bags of garbage on top of him. Rico looked at all the men and gave a small nod.

The younger out of the four, which was really the rookie inmate, pushed the cart towards the caged main door. He slapped the control booth for the women to open the door. She popped the button and allowed him to push the rolling tubby inside before closing the door. The young goon gave Rico a slight nod and swiftly eased back to his room. The other three inmates did the same.

The silence in the dormitory was thicker than cement. It was the jungle. No cameras, no help, no surviving. When it came to playing against the business code, Detective Bradley was the fucking chairman. There was nothing he couldn't do, nor anywhere he couldn't go when it involved Wilmington. The table was displeased with Cheek's actions, so he had knocked himself off of the chess board. That duty was now passed down to Ryan, who was surely gonna comply or receive the same fate.

* * *

Severe, Detective Bradley's duck-off restaurant

The small steakhouse was down in the bottom of Delaware. The plain Jane set-up would trick you if you didn't actually take the time to go with the opposite thought in your mind. The food was banging, and all the old heads around the city could be found posted Monday through Thursday. Today was a Sunday, so the full parking lot was a lot smaller than usual.

Severe strolled inside and made sure that his waves were on point. There was never no telling when a bitch wanted to be a flunky for the movement, so every second counted. The small establishment made it easy for him to spot Detective Bradley sitting in the corner of the eatery. Only a couple of guests roamed around and gossiped while chowing on some good-ass steaks.

Easing over to the table, Severe took a seat in the chair that was directly across from him. Detective Bradley raised his head from the plate and held up a finger. Taking one last bite of the delicious meal, he set down his fork and wiped his hand with a paper napkin. "So what's the issue? I've been working my ass off at the station, so minor shit is not gonna make me budge."

Severe waved the remark off. "I'm only here to make sure that what we agreed to is still on the table. I been handling my end, and I'm gonna handle the rest when I'm sure that you're on the same page as me."

"And what page are you on?" Detective Bradley sat back and stared at Severe with a tedious expression.

"The weight. I get to keep whatever I touch, but what about the money? I'm damn sure not just settling for the side change. I need to make sure that I'm going to be good, Bradley."

"You'll be good if shit plays out correctly, motherfucker. This ain't no interview, son. It's no more agreements, and it's quite clear what will happen when we receive everything that's in the agreement. It's easy. All you have to do is wait for my call, and be ready."

Chuckling, Severe intertwined his fingers like he was a true businessman. He leaned forward and squinted his eyes to make sure he was being felt. "I'm risking my damn life to make this shit happen. I ain't never failed at nothing I've been put on. You know what's at hand, so when it comes down to the main event, I wanna see action."

Detective Bradley pulled ten dollars from his wallet and tossed it on the table. "Once you begin to listen, you can elevate. Make sure you do it right instead of rushing, because the same way things can go right, they can also go horribly wrong, and that'll point the fingers back down to you, son. Don't just speak about that real shit, 'cause a lot of niggas behind the wall was built for this shit too. We all know after that pressure starts to be applied, a weak one will break within the first thirty seconds. So let's not play hard instead of smart. Lay low, wait for my call, and leave it at that." He stood to leave.

Severe eyed him with a slight attitude and stood up with him. "I'm not slipping on nothing, Bradley. When

I come, I'm coming correct, so the speech shouldn't be for me. It was supposed to be applied to the ones before me. I'll be in touch." Severe smirked and exited the restaurant.

Severe headed back across the street to his whip. He climbed in and glanced over to Detective Bradley, who was standing in the parking lot with a stale look. Severe flashed him a thumbs up before he pulled away from the scene. A mission was set out to be done, and it was getting handled with or without the help of anyone. Ryan and his little team were in the way of his path, and that shit was about to part like a *Soul Train* line. The city of Delaware wasn't big enough for too many different brains. It would always be the simple shit that a nigga executed to conquer it all. It was the only way Severe was coming. Quiet and randomly. The hourglass was now decreasing.

Chapter 11

Club Royal (Ryan's club)

Precious moved around the club, passing out small free drinks to the packed floor. Tonight was a special secret event. It was a fundraiser to push Club Royal up to new heights. She was networking and stacking grand plans to have Ryan's business at the top. It was hard getting a bigger building and packing it out with a whole bunch of party animals. A new investor showed up to the club and could see the strong vision in Precious's mind. There was much potential in the live spot, and if the money man understood that, she was going to push every night to the limit. He was going to write the check for her without hesitation.

The loud crowd was stomping around and bobbing to the new single from Young Thug's mixtape. So much fun. Her female assistants walked around with matching sexy black designer dresses she had purchased the day before. Appetizers were available for the hungry in case one got a little too tipsy, and the drinks were flowing nonstop. The aura was so unique. She wished that Ryan could have laid eyes on the way his shit was booming tonight. The work life placed you in matters where you would have to miss certain things for bigger opportunities. His strong ambition was what caused her to lock on with his great energy. Regardless of how hard he seemed, Ryan showed Precious a different side, the side that wanted success in bold letters. He just had a bad problem with asking for a helping hand, and that's where her job came in. All Ryan had to do was place his trust within her, and she would eventually make him one of the happiest men to ever invest with her. Maybe even for a little more, she thought before jumping back to work mode.

Reckless walked smoothly through the front entrance with five street thugs accompanying him. The security outside was more bitch than man, and there wasn't a better place to catch a nigga than a small-ass club that boasted your last name like you were related to the fucking Prince of England. The bitch made stunt that Ryan and DJ tried to pull out on the block was proof that they knew. They were so pussy-whipped that Reckless didn't want to waste the hard energy on checking the temperature. If they were pulling up from Philly down on the block, they damn sure didn't want to talk.

Reckless moved with his small crew to the reserved area and walked straight through the fake ass rope that stretched across the small entrance.

A brown-skinned man with a small Mohawk quickly stepped forward. A bottle of Remy was in one hand, and his phone was in the other. Before Reckless and them could began to pop their shit, the man stepped in between them.

"Excuse me, fellas, this section is bought for tonight. You can't just buck and walk past the rope. I need you fellas to leave immediately."

Reckless began to break down a White Owl cigarillo and laughed. "Nigga, we ain't going nowhere. This our section now."

The man placed his phone inside his pants pocket. "I'm gonna say it one last time. You guys need to get up and leave."

Instead of getting a reply with words, one of Reckless's goons punched the small man in his chin, knocking him out with one hit. The guests in the VIP watched as he crashed over the small drinking tables.

"You see what that talking get ya." Reckless sparked his blunt and exhaled a cloud of smoke.

Certain people looked on to see if they could get a view of what was going on. It didn't take long for Precious to see the movements and walk across the room, where she spotted Reckless and his team leaning and rocking to the music. A group of people was trying to help the poor man off the floor so he could receive medical assistance. A few of the shooters laughed as they watched the little dude stumble to his feet.

Precious wasted no time making her way up the small steps to approach the problem directly. Walking up to Reckless, she tapped his shoulder. "Excuse me, sir. I'm the owner, and it seems that we're having a problem with you men inside of our business. I'm gonna have to ask you gentlemen to leave. We don't want any problems, but we run a business, not a gambling spot."

"Damn, do we get a number if we comply?" one of Reckless's men asked stepping a little too close to her.

Precious moved slightly back and pulled out her cell phone. "Am I gonna have to call the police to handle this? Because they don't have a problem stopping by. The station sits like five minutes away," she warned, showing those fat-ass three digits on her phone screen.

Reckless stood to his feet and moved his young hoodlum out of the way. "Oh, you his little side piece, ain't you? I didn't know that ass was fat like that." He looked down at her voluptuous behind in that tight-ass dress. "What's good with you?"

"Nothing but the front door that all six of you troublemakers need to be leaving out of." Precious pointed like an elementary school teacher.

Reckless held up his hands in a submissive manner. The music had been lowered, and the two bodyguards who were controlling the front door were now standing a few feet away from the VIP in case something needed to be handled. That still didn't stop Reckless from proceeding with his plan. Leaning closer to Precious. He glared into her gorgeous eyes.

"Your man needs to come see me, because I don't wanna have to shoot up y'all little spot every night. This was only my warning," he mumbled before nodding to his accomplices.

The five men began to trash the club, using whatever they could. Tables were being kicked over. Chairs were being thrown. One of the men slashed the speakers until the inside was out.

Looking on in horror, Precious jolted her head back at the scary-ass security guards who stood there like they were more nervous than she was.

"Just leave my business, please!" she yelled, trying to stop the small rampage.

People were quickly exiting the building, and the bandits moved all the way towards the front door, breaking whatever sat in their path. They even swung on a few men who were standing to the side with their eyes roaming for descriptions. The tragedy eventually came to an end when they decided to exit the club and leave.

A few people sat around wondering what the hell just took place. The vibe was so live, and a group of dudes arrived and turned it upside down. The mentioning of Ryan's name gave Precious a clearer picture of what was going on. It was obviously one of those bad blood relationships that was about to start spreading towards the safety of every person who was attending Precious's crafty event.

She looked at all the small damage around the area. She instantly used her phone to call Ryan. His answer was quicker than usual because he answered on the second ring.

"What's good, love?"

"Ryan, we have a problem. I need you to get down to the club now." Her voice was irritated and shaken.

"What's wrong?"

She turned her back to the small crowd and spoke through the line. "This guy you're having problems with. He just showed up with five other dick heads and started causing drama. I tried to ask them to leave, and he laughed. After, he told me that he was only here for you. It wasn't even a few minutes after when they began to destroy the club."

"I'm on the way." He hung up in a rush.

Precious stared at the blinking screen. She exhaled and started to make her way around the club to check on the people who didn't rush out. Precious didn't have a gangsta bone in her body, but she was strong naturally by her heart. She truly felt that common courtesy made the world push around.

Unfortunately, those ways of thinking were nonexistent these days. All she could think about was the men reappearing to cause more damage, or worse, take a life.

Chapter 12

After getting Precious's call, Ryan abandoned his plans and chose to lay back like DJ said. That thought went out the window when he heard the news of Reckless making the stupid-ass mistake. Not only was Ryan gonna kill him, he was going to make an example. This would be the first friend of his to be killed in front of every possible citizen. Reckless was the live and die type nigga when he tested the sea, but he could never accept that one day a bigger prey could arrive, and he would become the feast.

Ryan and DJ reached the club about twenty minutes after Precious's call. The only problem was the thick blue and red lights that glistened brightly. That bitch looked like a cop's funeral. There was no way in fuck he was pulling inside of that club to receive the third degree from authorities. The police in Delaware were true assholes by nature. It was a no-win situation because they needed the extra money, even around tax time. A seventeen-year-old with an Infiniti truck would be like a big steak and a beer to them.

"Are you just gonna wait until she calls you? Those people ain't going nowhere any time soon." DJ leaned against the car door. They had been parked down the street for about thirty minutes, and the police still hadn't made a move yet.

"Of course I'm gonna wait. I'm not about to clash with these bum-ass cops because they don't wanna see a young hustler who matches the image. All I'm worried about is her. Precious is a suburb chick, man. I can't allow this girl to get hurt on my watch when she's worked so hard to build the little shit I do got." Ryan paced back and forth to try and calm himself.

"Word. We have to make sure she good, but this is the time to start thinking, bro. Maybe you should move a little more low-key. Switch cars, and allow other people to move for you. It's no way to be a person you can't see. I don't wanna see this idiot get you a life sentence for biting his bait. I've never seen him act like this, and I can't even think about telling you to spare him after pulling this shit, but I will tell you to be smart. Get his ass touched, and leave it at that. No blood on your hands, and you still make your money in peace." DJ eyed Ryan as he moved back and forth.

"He just hating. I got the money. I got the reputation." Ryan patted his chest like that would prove his words to be authentic. "If these niggas would have just listened, Wicked wouldn't be locked down, and this clown could be eating with us. It's like he wants to die."

"He does, nigga, but that don't mean we gotta do it. I'll be off to school soon, and you will be sitting somewhere in the next few months living the life with the shit you earned. Reckless's ass will be in a box choking in dirt, and Delaware will place him in the book as a crash dummy. This is Wilmington, Ryan. Everybody knows who's been putting in that work, and it ain't the two cousins from Arizona," DJ said truthfully.

Ryan knew those were facts. After meeting the two identical relatives a few years back, he had linked with them and eventually added DJ to the bunch. It was around the sixth grade school year when they all crossed paths and decided to lock in their brotherhood forever. He never thought that one day shit would go downhill. They were supposed to have an unbreakable bond, the love that would get you and your family buried alive about my brother type loyalty.

"No one is in control of how a person wakes up and thinks, but my mind is not built for dealing with shit like this. Why can't everybody follow the tracks if we paved it for them?"

"Because everybody don't think like you, Ryan. You different. I'm different," DJ stressed. "We got to worry about the things that's most important. Faith, and Prince need you, bro."

Hearing his child's mother's name, he thought back to the message he sent to her this morning after the meeting with Richard. He was so busy making the paper that he didn't even have the time to stop and pick up his own seed. The blame was placed on him regardless of how hard he tried. Faith was just too much, and she would be the main one to divert him from getting to the dough. It was the reason he placed so much distance in between them. Change was something that he just wasn't ready for. No one knew how shit would flip when you were living paycheck to paycheck. He didn't want Prince to suffer the same way as he did coming up. Ryan would rather miss this small amount of time with his son in order to be there every day for his bright future.

"You right, bro, but I really need your help with this shit. You help me hold it all together. I know what you about to venture off with when you hit school in a few months, so I wanna get you all the loot I can so you won't never have to worry. After you gone, I'll push on and find another way to spend my time. I just gotta know that you supporting me until you get the hell on. I ain't got no one else." Ryan looked his friend in the eyes with sincerity.

DJ wanted to deny the promise because there was no telling how he could wake up feeling the next day. Ryan was his boy, and he had always stood with him through whatever. It wouldn't be right to turn his right hand down after their past history. "I got you, bro. All we have to do is move smart and take shit slow. I'm gonna be right here," he assured him before Ryan's phone began to ring.

Precious's number was flashing across his screen, so he prepared himself to see whatever the verdict was. "Hey ma. What's going on?"

"The police are saying that they're going to start patrolling the area more to ensure that things like this don't occur. I didn't want to say the wrong thing, so I explained the basics to cover our back," she explained.

"Good. Are you okay?"

"Yeah, just a little shaken up. I guess I'm going to shut down and call it a night." Her voice sounded defeated.

"I want you to come home with me after you're finished. I'll be at the house waiting. We need to talk," Ryan requested.

"Okay. I'll be right over," she agreed

"Cool," Ryan said before hanging up.

DJ still posted against the car as if he was pondering something. Ryan broke his trance with a nudge on the shoulder. "You good, bro?"

"Yeah, just evaluating like always. Is Precious straight?" he quickly flipped the question.

"Yeah, she a'ight. I'm about to meet up with her in a second. I know you've been on a mission with me all day, so I'm gonna drop you off at home to get some rest. I know a break is needed after certain shit. I can come get you in the morning to see what we will do from there." Ryan walked to the driver side of his car.

"Yeah, I do need a rest." DJ followed and got inside of the car.

Before Ryan started the car, he looked over to his friend. "I just wanna thank you for keeping it solid with me, bro. That means a lot."

"Stop being sentimental, nigga. That's what homies are for." He rested his eyes and leaned back in the seat.

Ryan smiled before starting the engine, and exited the parking lot. The respect that he shared for his boy stretched a mile long. Not only were those feelings mutual, but it felt good to know when you could count on a person that claimed to be there forever. DJ was the friend that Ryan knew would be there, right or wrong.

Or so he thought.

Chris Green

Chapter 13

Precious was laughing hard at the comedy movie playing on Ryan's flat screen. It felt good to see her sexy ass smile. Her beauty was a magnet, and she was surely a girl that any man would dream of spitting their little babies in.

Ryan couldn't help but to gaze at her. After meeting up with him, he did his best to ease her tension from the incident that occurred earlier. The way she was explaining the story made him ponder killing Reckless the same night. The idiot was declaring war with a fool who didn't truly know anything else but murder. Once the time began to roll, he and Precious started to lay back and relax which resulted in them finding a classic on the Hulu box.

Noticing that he was staring at her, Precious flashed him a cheesy grin. "What?"

"Nothing. I'm just looking." His pupils roamed up and down her body slowly like she was prey on a tiger's menu. Her ass was so soft that it shifted with every small movement she made. Her breasts were perky and plump, and the gorgeous eyes on her face would make you fall weak and bust within a few seconds. Ryan lusted in his mind, but his mouth wouldn't allow him to express shit of that nature.

"It looks like you wanna attack me," she mumbled in a sexy voice before cutting her eyes back at the TV. She was trying to change the station in her mind because her emotions between her thighs lightly tingled. Ryan's energy was so thick that she could still feel him staring. Turning to meet his eyes again, she smirked. "You must wanna fight?"

"Nah," he answered, stroking her cheek with the back of his hand. The mystery in her eyes was so mind-boggling. Her heart spoke a message that he couldn't decode. She was always bouncing a steamy vibe on him without even trying. Ryan could tell that he was making her uneasy because she struggled to hold eye contact. "I know that I never told you this, but I really appreciate you being in my life. I truly feel that you're my angel." He flashed a handsome smile.

"Aww, Ryan, I'm always grateful to help and be here with you." Her cheeks showed those deep-ass dimples, sending his manhood a signal.

Ryan's heart pumped at a fast pace when she started to shift on the couch to match his gaze. She was a nerdy dime piece that didn't know much about the gangsta shit, but hoarded great facts about the streets. It was major turn on, one that he had never experienced with any other woman. For some reason, he just wanted to please her, and he still couldn't put enough reasons in his head why. Precious was an addictive energy that he craved. It was a different feeling when you could sense that shit in your soul about someone, and she wasn't his woman, which made him study her a little closer. Every second that passed while he stared deeply into her eyes felt like a Kodak moment that would last a million years.

Ryan couldn't help himself. His head said to go for it. Leaning slowly over to her, he kissed her passionately. As their lips intertwined, he could feel her tight body loosen in satisfaction. Her pink lips were soothing and soft. He could taste the minty flavor of her gum she had smacked in earlier, and his hands couldn't help but to slide down on caress her phat apple bottom. "I love you. If I do this, then you gotta be mines." He was nibbling on her ear as he whispered.

Precious's words were caught inside her throat. She panted from his statement. Just from the sound of his voice, she could tell that he was dead-ass serious. His fingers roamed her body gently before sliding her black dress up.

"Ryan." Precious shook nervously. "I don't wanna lose you as a friend. It's really hard to find friends. I've been let down to many times." She kissed his lips again.

Ryan stood up and removed his white T-shirt. Removing his Calvin Klein sweatpants, Precious roamed his body with 20/20 vision, and her body was ready to receive his next action. Ryan was back over her body within seconds. His naked body forced her to loosen up quickly. Her lips quivered because Ryan had a look that said he was about to beat her pretty pussy into submission.

Ryan spread her legs and instantly went down between her thighs for his specialty. Precious's chest began to rise in anticipation. Wrapping his lips around her kitty, he wasted no time sucking on the little button lightly. As he thrust his tongue forward, Precious moaned lightly with a small shiver. Her body was warm and soft. The tone of her skin color demanded attention through the dimmed living room. Her womanhood was his antidote, and he could feel himself attach to her with every lick he delivered.

Ryan ran his tongue up and down her plump vagina. She raised her head to watch his mouth punk her out. With every lick, he delivered a kiss, and his hands gently caressed her inner thighs slowly. The first orgasm began to rise after he slid his tongue inside of her pussy. Precious's eyes rolled and her back was arched, expressing her sensation. It was coming. The tingle of his lips was sliding around her smoothly, and her pussy pulsated, sending a hypnotizing feeling over her body.

"Don't change on me, Ryan." Her voice rolled angelically through his earlobe.

Mounting her body, Ryan bit down on her neck. His manhood was harder than a brick. Precious could feel the tip gently rubbing across her lips until it reached her tight entrance. Precious pouted lightly as he slowly pushed his way into her small hole. The tension in her body was contracting with every inch he placed inside.

"Ryannn, please don't hurt me. Just love me," she begged while gripping her breasts.

Ryan placed his forehead directly against hers and slid deeper. Her pussy didn't hesitate to soak from his perfect rhythm. Rising on his fist, he sped up his rhythm. Precious's tone slightly rose with every stroke. Her juices were covering the head of his rod brightly. Not only was she warm, but her kitty was more than tight. The loud sound of her sweet spot being penetrated roamed through the air, and it enticed him to make more time, be gentler. That pussy was speaking in different languages, especially when he gripped her hips.

Ryan's size was magnificent. His touch was like no other. Sparkles in her eyes would shine every time he filled her completely.

"You was made for me." Ryan kissed her face. His tongue glided lightly across her bottom lip, and his dick felt as if it was sitting in her tummy.

"It's so deep, Ryan. It's deep," she pleaded with light pinches to his side.

Sliding out of her, he rolled her over and hiked her leg up for easy access to that pretty peach. Her body was floating, and her moans were still ringing from the last orgasm he just bestowed upon her. Precious could feel his hands sliding across her soft bubble butt. Her flawless arch placed a messy scene in Ryan's head. It was time to stamp that pussy with a big daddy lesson. He eased back in her goodies. Her booty moved like a gentle wave in the ocean. The sound of her wet treat was sounding off after he dug in with his first pump. Precious quivered lightly and covered her mouth. The position she was in allowed him to have all the pleasure of her creamy scene that was about to happen within the next few seconds.

"Fuck, baby." He was mugging while sliding that dick deeply in her guts. Her soft cheeks collided across his pelvis when he started to place his pound game down. Locking in her shoulder with his right arm, he plunged between her cheeks deeply,

"Oh my God, Ryan!" Precious cringed, feeling that thunder drop inside her body.

Ryan was in heaven. Precious was hands down the best woman he'd ever wrapped his arms around. Her sex was making him feel as if she was already a part of his new world. The more he stroked, the wetter she became.

"Ryan, I'm cumm-" She paused as the sensation exploded. The white cream slowly began to drip from her pussy lips.

Ryan glanced at the beautiful sight and smeared it across her ass with his two middle fingers. Her ass was all he could focus on. It clapped louder when he focused on her slippery spot. Precious's long hair complemented her gorgeous sex face. The expression she was showing made him want to ease up with the deep back shots, but her body was forcing his pipe to react differently. She was trying to take that shit like a gutta bitch, but her pouty lips exposed the suburb beauty that needed to be claimed. She needed a man that was gonna show how things would go. Hiking his right leg up being her, Ryan dug balls deep into her vagina.

"I can't breathe, daddy," she panted when he began to land more strikes deeply inside of her gushy sweetness.

Within seconds, she could feel Ryan's posture tighten. His nut was about to cum, and his passionate expression told the pain he was about to release. Spreading her ass cheeks with a firm grip, he watched his dick pump forcefully inside of her. His mind was so obsessed with Precious's loveable personality. He didn't flinch when his dick exploded in her tight kitty. Ryan gave her a few more slow, deep-ass strokes while kissing her back gently.

"I share a love for you that I can't explain," Ryan grunted lightly as he eased slowly out of her.

Turning on her side, Precious laid gently against the soft couch. Beads of sweat rolled down her back and beautiful face. Her eyes were squinting from the tingling pulse that was bumping inside of her womanhood. "You showed me." She leaned up to peck his lips. Her eyes gave him the clear indication that she was surely gonna prove her loyalty.

Returning her freaky-ass kiss, his eyes molested her banging-ass body. Not only was he marking his territory, Ryan was thinking about a few more freaky-ass ways to please a twenty-six-year-old woman. His fingers rubbed up and down her slippery split gently.

Precious was so drained. All she could do was cock her legs wider to offer a full view of her treasure.

"Precious, I don't know how you feel about your personal life, or if you had someone else working on getting to know you. You don't need that anymore. I will be the first and last nigga to touch you after this day," he spoke lightly while inching closer to her. His hands cuffed around her hips tightly.

"Are you sure about what you're saying, Ryan? What makes you think that you will settle for a girl like me?" she mumbled shyly. Her gorgeous-ass face showed the innocence that flowed through her veins. She was major respectful with a blessed body.

"You're the most beautiful girl I've ever laid my hands and eyes on. You have a natural glow that makes me just wanna hold and please you in the nastiest way possible." His hands gripped both of her soft ass cheeks.

Blushing, she wrapped her smooth leg around him. "It feels good to see you actually have this in your heart. You're have grown heavily on me within these few months of our encounter. "You say that I belong to you. My Hulu movie is not worth more than me stare at you connecting with me so good." Her hand stroked his dick, instantly bricking him back up. Trailing her fingers up his chest, she kissed him. "I'll oblige with whatever you say to me. Don't hurt me, and never stop satisfying your ambitions to be better. I'll be right there every day if that's what you want." She was glancing down every other second at his stiff thick meat with a seductive eye.

Ryan knew that her oven was heating back up, and he didn't know exactly how things would go between their new plans for building. Her mind was focused, and she was able to act at the necessary times how a real ride or die should. That was all Precious had to remember, because she carried the missing pieces on her back when they crossed paths the very first time.

"You sure that I'm what you want?" They embraced with a deep kiss before she could answer. After their lips unlocked, she bit on her bottom lip.

"So do you think this is what you want?"

Ryan searched her face to get that sexy-ass look out of her. Raising from under his arm, she stretched out on the floor and arched her ass directly in the air. "Can you pull that same energy again? I want it just like the first round," she giggled with a sneaky-ass grin.

Of course the flawless-ass image she was flashing made his dick jump in excitement. Ryan made his way to the living room floor behind her. He stroked his dick numerous times until he was able to slide in her with a firm deep shot like she truly craved.

"Yes, baby. That's it!" She gritted on her teeth when his fingertips sank into her booty.

Ryan's shit was still in effect from the last round, and he felt so huge pumping with force between her walls. When her face buried into the living room carpet, he knew that it was about to be a long night. Biting his bottom lip, Ryan calmed down and began to deliver his hard sweet pound game once again. The house was clear for her to be pleased in whatever section or room Ryan chose. His balls slapping against her backside forced Precious's ass to jiggle forcefully against his pulsating dick. Precious moaned loudly and looked back at him with the sexiest look she could muster. Blocking out the mercy shit, he proceeded to slam in that shit with all nine.

Precious's tongue rolled around, and she could feel Ryan hitting low. She hiked her ass a tad bit higher. He smiled, knowing that it was about to be a long, nasty-ass night with her. He slapped Precious's ass with a hard right hand, making it quake. That hot-ass tension was cooking up, and Ryan just couldn't resist her, He was about to fuck until she really felt the meaning of his love. No one was gonna explore Precious the way he handled himself in the sheets. It was creating the mold to his new future. Precious was his wife already and didn't have the slightest clue.

Chris Green

Chapter 14

10:23 a.m.

After awakening and handling his business the following morning, Ryan dropped DJ's complaining ass off and headed back to the spot for Precious. Her last three nights were spent inside of his bed - and all over the furniture of his home, of course. It was major time with bonding and doing the freakiest shit they could think of. It wasn't long before Ryan reached the crib, and when he arrived, she didn't hesitate to strip naked. The room would be heated once he got started, and raw sex was turning him into a pure addict for how she matched his sex cravings. Once his lovemaking duties were done, Precious fell into a deep sleep within minutes.

Ryan slid out of the bed and tossed on his sweats to hit the kitchen. He reached his mark and opened the fridge. He was preparing to grab the orange juice when his doorbell rang. Ryan leaned up quickly and checked the time on his watch, reaching for the 9mm pistol under the cabinet. He placed one in the chamber and walked towards the door. The bell sounded two more times before he could open it.

Faith was standing on the other side of his door posted with an attitude.

"Faith, what are you doing here? What did I tell you about just showing up?" Ryan shook his head in exhaustion.

"Ryan, yo' ass act like you can't even come sit with me and your child for one day, so you shouldn't be mad about my driving or pulling up on you for these little fifteen minutes. I'm coming to let you know that if you ain't tightened up within the next few days, I'm filing for child support and cutting all ties until you decide to be a dad, bitch." Faith was shifting her head from side to side as if she had that threat plotted for days.

"Who the fuck are you calling a bitch? Faith, you asking to get yo' ass beat with all the greasy talk. Relax, and get the fuck back across that damn bridge before I punch you out." He moved to close the door in her face, but she used her foot to block his ass.

"Ryan, I'm not playing with you. I've gave you nothing but respect, and I see that you've gotten too big in order to feel some pain, baby daddy. You know I'll act out, Ryan. I don't care about you trying to fight me or none of that shit. My child isn't a Louie bag, nigga. You not about to pick him up when you feel like it, but not keep your word with the shit that comes out of your own mouth!" she yelled. "I didn't have a baby so you could dog me. You can't even give me a reason why you left, Ryan." Her voice was starting to break up, but she refused to cry and let him win.

Ryan was about to explode until Precious stepped into the living room with a small notepad. She instantly locked eyes with Faith, but didn't say anything. Ryan knew that he couldn't even waste him time to explain, so the awkward silence continued until Faith laughed and shook her head at Ryan.

"I guess this was the business partner that you was referring to. She looks good and comfortable sliding out of your room ass naked."

Ryan shrugged his shoulders. "Thanks. Maybe I can get her to go back in there if you please leave.

There ain't nothing here for you. What's so hard to understand?"

That fuck-ass comment cut Faith deep. The one thing she always trusted in her mind was Ryan loving her for eternity. All that same time, the love was all being thrown out the window because of his own desires, which made it even more pathetic. "So is this because of you earning a few dollars in the neighborhood, or because you wanted to be this way from the start, Ryan?"

Precious stood against the wall, silently waiting to see how things were about to play out.

Faith raised her voice a little louder to get Ryan's attention. "Ryan Royal, I'm speaking to you. How do I explain something like this to our son?" She folded her arms in search of an answer.

Ryan gazed into her eyes with pity and said the hardest thing in his life. "You're not the one for me, Faith. I'll take care of my son, but there ain't nothing else between me and you. I'm sorry," he admitted.

The phony smile on Faith's face was only a symbol of hatred. His mind couldn't even imagine the crazy shit that was rushing through her brain. Before she shed any tears down her face, she sucked her emotions down and walked away. Whatever fake-ass love she dedicated between her and Ryan was smashed. He cut a slice so deep from her mind and spirit. That was a personal pain, a sick pain that she was about to experience before her love chapter could even start. Ryan caused so much trauma, and she would still defend his honor because of the bond they shared.

Now it was clear that he wanted to play for keeps and toy with the wrong heart - a heart that wouldn't accept being ticked with.

The door behind her closed loudly before she even reached the bottom of his steps. She climbed in the small car, lowered her head in defeat, and cursed. She sat a short moment before starting the engine to make her way back to Wilmington.

Chapter 15

Wilmington County sheriff's office

Reckless was furious as he paced around the small holding cell. About two hours ago, he was snatched up by the authorities and tossed in the back of a police cruiser. No one even cared to read him his Miranda rights or give him a clear explanation on why he was being arrested. After being held for close to an hour, he received the news of the warrant on his name for eluding the police. His name was being placed inside of three recent shootings, and the authorities wanted him scooped for questioning immediately. The only good news he received was about the bond fee for his charge. It was a little high, but all he needed was someone to handle the business with the bonding company so he could be released, and he could leave the city for a few weeks. Jail wasn't even an option. There was too much going on, including the task of taking what he was owed.

Reckless watched as a black officer entered the small holding area. His eyes were scanning over a blue file folder, obviously previous history papers on Reckless. The detective walked slowly passed the row of cell tanks and stopped directly in front of his door.

"So Mr. Samson, we've gotten numerous calls about you acting illiterate around my motherfucking city. Lucky for you, the county that wants you for investigation isn't coming to get you no time soon. If you're here for more than a week, I'll transfer you over to the institution for an appearance in court." He closed the file like there was no such thing as debating.

"So what will happen if I bond out?" he asked through the thick glass. "I can't stay here. I'm the provider for my family," he lied with a straight face.

"If you're not able to get a guardian for a bond signature, it's over. You'll need ten thousand dollars, or some property that's worth four times that value. You'll be able to make a call in about twenty minutes. You might wanna take the time figuring out who's the best person to help you, Mr. Samson," the detective confirmed.

Nodding with understanding, Reckless moved back to the steel bench and took a seat. No one was willing to come lend him ten thousand dollars, and he damn sure didn't have any property to place up. The recent cash he was splurging with was squandered on bullshit so hits pockets were back on empty besides the four hundred bucks that was in his pocket. If he couldn't handle the shit fast. He was surely gonna ride out for a bid if his face appeared inside of another courtroom. His mind pondered on one person that could possibly save the day for him to walk out of those cuffs. He just wasn't sure if it would be guaranteed.

Chapter 16

North Philly, Frankford Avenue

Coming out of the block's corner store, Ryan listened to Torey spill the beans on his former problem. It was amazing how shit could play out for a person who walked crooked. Words could spread like wildfires, and karma was a true bitch.

Ryan jumped into his car and quickly cut Torey off mid-sentence. "Listen, cuz. I just need that handled whenever possible. I hate distractions, and I'm going above these little niggas very soon. I don't have time for games, and I can't take chances on people who act out with disrespect."

"Ryan, just stop. This is my hobby, bro. Let me be the expert, and you worry about making these big dreams happen. I got the shit under control, but you gotta trust me. I got a plan, and I bet it's going to work. Don't make it more complicated," Torey spoke with confidence.

Ryan could tell by his cousin's calm attitude that his word was bond. It was mutual, and family was meant to trust family until they showed otherwise. "Thanks, cuz. I'll send the first half your way in about one hour. Watch out for my call."

"I should be telling you that," Torey responded before ending the call.

Ryan shook his head from the crazy remark and chuckled. Torey wasn't going to stop being an asshole for anyone - not even himself. The only thing he respected was his cousin's word. He could handle business accordingly, which eased a load from Ryan's shoulders.

Just as he was about to pull away from the curb, Kimyetta's name flashed across his cell phone. It had been a while since he got a chance to hear her voice. It was call that he couldn't pass up. Answering, he placed the phone up to his ear. "Ma."

"Don't 'Ma' me, boy. What the hell are you doing?" She checked his ass before he tried to butter her up.

Ryan couldn't help but to smile from ear to ear. "I miss you too, Ma. How you been?"

"Boy, quit lying. I'm gonna always be doing okay. I know how to move around with sticking my face in the wrong shit. I can't say the same thing about you."

"What do you mean?"

Kimyetta's voice shifted before rising through the receiver. "I know yo' big head ass heard me. I been hearing your damn name ringing like a fire truck. You still ain't learned, have you?"

Ryan exhaled, knowing where the conversation was about to lead. "Ma, I'm doing good, and my name ain't ringing like nothing. I'm just staying out of the way. How would you know what I'm doing if I'm alone up here? You left me, remember?"

"Ryan, didn't nobody leave yo' sorry ass. You just didn't have the courage to give that shit up and leave with me. You're not a baby no mo', and the streets pumping some different shit up there in that little brain of yours. I'm not supporting you with some shit that'll take you away." Kimyetta kept her words clear and to the point.

Ryan watched the moving traffic bypass his car while thinking of a response. Not too much could be said when you were at odds with the one who birthed you. It was a lose-lose. "You're my mom. I don't see why you always gotta call acting like this. When are you not mad?"

"It's a difference, Ryan. I'm not mad. I'm disappointed. These niggas out here don't owe you nothing but a few lies and a bullet. It's what I've seen my entire life, down from your granddaddy and father. It's spilled inside of you, and I have nightmares about me waking up to that painful phone call." Kimyetta's statement sounded like a desperate plea.

Ryan knew that all the advice he received through close people and relatives was the same thing Kimyetta continued to preach. Growing up in Delaware wasn't just a true test. It was a walk to manhood. If you could come out of the worst hood in Wilmington and conquer shit that took the average nigga forty years to do, it was destined. The game didn't just choose the player. It made its own rules, and even strategized a way to trap you in its grasp. Only a few could detect the signs and move the way necessary in order to win the grand prize at the end: freedom. That time wouldn't appear until a hundred million dropped inside of Ryan's lap.

"I understand, Mama. We gotta survive some kind of way though. You're my Queen in the end, and when I'm done with this life, at least I'll be able guarantee that I won't turn back. You still gotta love me," Ryan said sincerely. "I know how you are about this, and I'll always respect your words, Ma. Don't think I'm not listening."

"Whatever, Ryan. You don't love me, 'cause if you did, I wouldn't be by my damn self in a new home. I'll believe that when you standing in front of me," Kimyetta said before hanging up.

Ryan set the phone in his passenger seat and pulled away from the curb. As he blended in with the traffic, his mind wandered about the outcome of his life in the end. Sure, it took losses in order to become a beast with your craft. Those were the basics of the world. Some were born professionals, and others worked to become relevant to the society. Ryan knew that there was a possibility for a black man. All he had to do was put in the effort to make it possible. That was balance.

Thinking about his mom's request, he smiled. It felt good to know that she thought about him being with her. That was more motivation to get his bag right. His birthday was quickly approaching, and the check needed to be in the safe before the time presented itself. He was pushing for the millionaire's club. That would be the day that Kimyetta would be surprised for sure. He was gonna walk away and take her across the world to finally feel freedom.

Chapter 17

Nightfall was finally stretched across the sky, and the lights were shining bright to give a slight sign of life for the dangerous city. Ryan cruised around in his whip doing the half the dash and on his fourth cup of vodka. Within two hours, he pulled down on six different turfs and locked in with a few great connections. Precious was busy at school until tomorrow, and DJ was preparing to fill out all his fresh papers for that big-ass school in Jersey. Since he was rolling alone, it was smart to slide down on everyone he could. Within weeks, Ryan had collected so much money that his lips wouldn't even tell Kimyetta how much. It just wasn't his goal price.

Deja vu flashed and his phone began to ring like a few hours earlier while he was in traffic. Without checking the screen, Ryan answered with a slur. "Yooo, who the fuck is this?"

The operator for a prison began to speak, explaining how to accept a call. Ryan could barely here the instructions, but he did hear the number five. Wasting no time, he pressed the button to skip all the annoying fuckery.

The woman spoke once more, announcing that the call was now connected.

"Hello?" Ryan yelled a little too loudly.

"What's up, bro? How you feeling, big dawg?" the voice spoke through the line smoothly.

"Wicked?" Ryan had to straighten his posture to be sure that he wasn't too drunk.

"Yeah. It took me a while to get in contact, but I've been laying low, my guy. I wasn't even in the detention center a month before they offered me a deal for one year. I took that shit and ran, bro. Really didn't have a choice," Wicked tried to explain. The last move Reckless pulled caused him to catch a bid, and all he could do was accept it. His high school diploma was still being accepted and it was the only thing he could be thankful for at the time.

Ryan couldn't even force himself to be mad. For some reason, he always lowered his wing towards him. It was just the total opposite for Reckless. "We miss you out here, bro. I gave DJ some dough for you, and I know that shit may seem fucked up. But you still have real friends out here, my guy," Ryan said before tossing the small empty bottle of liquor out of his car window.

"Come on, man, ain't no other way. You remember that time where you took that nigga's book bag at school because his shit was better than mines? You made sure I wore that bitch every day til we got to Newark." Wicked laughed about the funny memory.

"I remember that shit. You had to be persistent, boy. I didn't beat that nigga up for no reason." Ryan cracked up before slowing down for the red light ahead.

"That shit was hilarious, man, that was definitely good times. I only had about fifteen minutes, but I wanted to call and let know that I ain't forgot about you, fool. You give me motivation through his shit. I ain't never had no mean-ass homie like you," Wicked said before the one minute indicator sounded off.

"Aye man, you can hit me up, bro. I'll send some more bread if you need it," Ryan offered.

"Nah, bro, just stay positive out there, and think. You gotta able to help me when I'm down, bro, but I'm not gonna beat yo' ears up. I'll scream at you when I can, bro," Wicked spoke with some good motivation.

"Always, man. I'll catch you later." Ryan hung up the line. His mind was still puzzled off the consumed liquor, and it felt like he had been driving around in circles for hours. Wicked's phone call was a surprise, and his convo was something to think about when Ryan heard the same shit daily. Constantly being warned of what not to do. Not being free. You couldn't fake love for the game because it possessed no soul. It was a giant Monopoly board running wild for the best business-minded individual to upload their new level of survival. The mind to save, when one would spend. The thought to invest, instead of making ties. Whoever set the mind to be good would receive the same amount back with progression. Life was pumping money through a printer faster than a bitch's coochie popping on the floor to Uncle Luke. Ryan wanted a portion - not all of it, just enough to spread around and do as the family pleased.

Busting a left down DJ's street, Ryan pulled down to his crib and parked his car in front of the crib. He tapped the horn twice. He pulled out his phone and scrolled down his Instagram to check his recent notifications.

DJ knocking on his window caused him to look up. Ryan popped the locks, allowing him to climb in the passenger seat.

"You can't just pull up on a nigga's whip, fool. Most niggas clapping off top." He smiled, showing DJ his new Springfield 45 automatic. A silencer was attached to the front with a small red beam.

"Nigga, where the fuck did you get that from? That shit look like a military gun." DJ grabbed it out of his hand to inspect it up close.

"Nah, it's not an army gun. I just know how to dress my bitch," Ryan bragged while reaching in the backseat to snatch up the large Jordan shoe box sitting in DJ's lap. Ryan grabbed his gun back. "This ain't for you, school boy. That is." He nodded to the grey box.

"Which ones you bought me, nigga? Cuz I ain't stepping out in nothing old." DJ slid off the top and smirked. A new Apple laptop sat inside with a roll of money on top. DJ couldn't help but to grab the cash first. "Is this a vacation bonus, boy? This shit kinda thick."

"That's ten grand, DJ. I won't you to start preparing for school early. The more we handle now, the less you have to deal with after enrollment." Ryan grabbed the laptop and examined it. "This too. It'll come in handy for all that fashion shit you 'bout to start."

"It's a clothing designer, ass." DJ died in laughter.

"Same thing. I know it'll come in handy, and there's more where that came from. It's just the beginning. You know I'm going to see Lucci next week. If I can keep this up and handle this shit accordingly, we're gonna walk off with millions - and I'm not talking about four or five." Ryan pulled another ten grand from his front pockets.

DJ stared at the cash with a joyous smile. He loved seeing his friend's ambition for getting his shit straight. "It was meant for you, Ryan. Nobody has a heart like you, so it's hard to compare your actions to anyone, but your honesty is what holds that shit up. You do straight up business, so the rest will respect it and fall in line."

Ryan clasped his hands together with a serious face. "I'm about to press every coin out of these bitches until the earth vibrates under my feet. I'm also about to fix a line between personal and business. If I make a decision about something, it's done. All I need is your brain for our estimation. The more cash, the more access." Ryan nodded.

DJ knew that shit was certainly real. It was normal to keep a little side dough, but not twenty G's. He could tell from Ryan's new appearance that his mind was building. Instead of the old sweat suits and jeans, he was now sporting two-piece tailored suits, collar shirts, and loafers, even designer pea coats. Ryan was really a young bull running half of Delaware because he chose to be. That was real respect that a nigga couldn't just step on.

"I'm right here, my nigga. These few months we have are about to be epic. Get the check, and let pawns move for us. No scene action unless it's necessary. Speaking of being noticed. Are you sliding down to Demerea's crib tomorrow for that party?" DJ asked.

"Party? I'm not good with shit like that, but I might. I'm just not with the drama. I just wanna lay back, fuck, and count." Ryan smirked arrogantly.

DJ dapped his boy up before thanking him again. "You know I appreciate you, Ryan. I'm gonna get my ass ready for bed and head to this campus for a walk around. It's gonna be weird as hell staying in some shit like that."

"That's what you signed up for. It happens when you elevate." Ryan checked the time on his watch. "I'll be making a few moves tomorrow so we can link up once all these affairs get handled."

"True. I'll check in once I'm back. Don't go looking for no pussy to buy at ten, o'clock either, nigga." DJ laughed before getting out of his truck.

"I don't mind if she thick with it!" Ryan yelled before turning on his stereo.

The loud bass from NBA Young Boy's hit "No Smoke" quaked through his speakers. The vibration under his feet was power to his mind. That's how he wanted people to feel when he came through. Like you needed to turn your head for a glimpse of his aura. A visual of the way he moved, and prospered with every step. Some people were gonna die losers, and that shit wasn't pumping nowhere in his body.

Swerving away from DJ's home, Ryan was sure to tuck his pistol on the side of his seat. The night was breezy and thick with adventure. It was about to be a solo night for Ryan, driving through the spot and networking with anybody stressing them checks. It was the only word he loved: hustle.

Chapter 18

9:00 a.m.

The calendar that read September 8, 2018 was all Reckless's eyes could see as he sat inside the cold-ass tank. After calling up Severe last night about helping with his bond, he received a dead tone. Knowing that the old head needed a shooter, Reckless was always ready to pull a favor for a favor. Once that route failed him, he tried a few more niggas that claimed to have all this imaginary-ass paperwork. Before he could find a savior to rescue him, the officer ended his phone time and placed his ass back in the cell with a sand which. It was the last time he received any interaction with an officer. All he needed to do was place a few more calls, before the weak-ass county decided to pick him up for a transfer.

Just as Reckless thought about kicking the steel door, one of the rookie officers entered the office and walked up to his tank.

"Mr. Samson. Your bond has been posted so we're about to process you out, sir. "

"What?

"Your bond sir. It's been paid in full. I'll try and have you out of here in about twenty minutes." He grabbed the file off of the wall and moved to the main desk.

Reckless couldn't believe what the hell he was hearing. Nothing could stop a real one from wagging through the cracks. Obviously, Severe must have re-played that cornball-ass proposition back and thought twice. It truly didn't matter because no one would be able to place him in a scale for rules and baby feeding-ass movements. He was willing to play around and make some paper with whoever was talking the best. His name for laying shit down was growing effortlessly. No one liked him, but didn't have enough guts to speak it publicly. His mind was prepared to lay some shit down the same night. Reckless pockets were on one, but it damn sho' didn't discourage him. You either ate or got eaten in Delaware, and he stood firmly on that shit.

After a few minutes of pacing around the six by nine, the officer was opening the cell door. Reckless walked out and grabbed the property bag from the pig's hand.

"How do I go by getting my money back that y'all took?"

The officer clipped the name band from his wrist and placed a piece of paper into his hand. "I'll tell you now, kid. That money's probably being spent on a hooker across town somewhere. There is no solution to that. Fill out the paper and place your signature on the line."

Roaming his eyes down the paper as if he was really viewing his terms of bond, Reckless snatched the pen from the man's hand and scribbled his name down. Folding it, he placed it back into the officer's hand.

"Thanks. Now move over to the front desk so we can get your prints. After that, you are free to go." The man waved his hand for him to follow.

The small holding center only held a certain amount of inmates. The only people who operated the floor were three sloppy body patrol guards and the secretary who was sitting behind the front desk.

"Ms. Williams. This is Mr. Samson. Can you fingerprint him to be released?" the scrawny police officer asked while reaching for a business card on the counter.

"Sure." She looked at Reckless and blushed. "Maybe next time you'll stay out of trouble."

"I'm not in trouble. They just hate me," he shot back as she guided his fingers one by one on the black ink box. Lifting his hand slowly, she pressed them down on a white chart sheet.

"No one hates you. They may dislike, but not hate. If no one has tried to kill you, got you thrown in prison, or beat up pretty bad, they might just envy something that they weren't blessed with. Take it as a compliment." She picked up the fingerprint sheet and passed him a paper napkin. "Try and stay away from the back of cop cars. It becomes addictive."

"I'll try." He grinned before making his way to the front door.

Upon getting to the front door, Reckless waited until the guard popped the locks for him to exit. He walked out of the main entrance and sniffed the morning air in delight. The wind was cutting a little strong, but it felt good to slide out of those cuffs.

Reckless stepped out into the small parking lot and decided to walk down to the nearest corner store. It was easy to call a cab and take the quick way home. As he strolled across the concrete in his own thoughts, a large black Yukon truck backed out of their parking space, nearly hitting him.

"Goddamn, man. Watch where the fuck you going, motherfucker! You like to hit me!" Reckless shouted while pointing at the driver's tinted window.

His mouth was about to shout out another slander until the front and back truck windows lowered down quickly. Torey and Free lifted from the truck, pointing their assault rifles with the looks of death engraved on their faces. Reckless's heart skipped a beat before he froze in place. The moment felt like he was stuck in slow motion. He heard the guns rack back and the first bullet releasing hitting him in the chest.

The feeling of that bullet snapped Reckless back to reality, and his last breath witnessed the rapid bullets that shredded his life within a few seconds.

When his body folded against the pavement, Torey hung out of the car window as his driver smashed off, leaving the smell of burned rubber lingering heavily.

The female desk clerk of the facility rushed from the building with her gun blazing at the Suburban. Boom! Boom! Boom! Boom! Boom!

One of her shots tagged the back window, shattering it to pieces, before the suspects quickly bent a hard right corner. Jumping on her radio, she requested back up and jogged over to Reckless. He was sprawled out on the ground with numerous gunshot wounds. His body was covered in blood, and you could see the horrific sight of Reckless's jaw slightly detached from the right side of his face.

Trembling from the scene, the officer turned her head and began to puke uncontrollably. The beautiful day she pictured flipped over to a dark nightmare for the station. There was a dead body in front of the building, and now the explanation of these mystery suspects was about to begin once Officer Williams spotted the backup units flooding down the street.

The road was blocked off in seconds, and numerous authorities leaped out of their cruisers, guns drawn for whatever threat presented itself. Glancing back over to Reckless's body. She placed a hand over her mouth and said a silent prayer for him before walking away to confront her commander.

Chris Green

Chapter 19

Ryan's spot, the northside of Philly

After hanging up the phone with Lucci Bruno, Ryan jumped to his feet with excitement. The money he was just offered would compensate him handsomely if the money added up fast enough for Richard. The twenty keys Lucci purchased last week was sent straight down the interstate towards Georgia, where they actually made the money that most drug dealers dreamed of. Lucci was not only an asset with his clientele, but also when it was time to travel, and visit other places. He would be a friend for life, if they could move the weight without fumbling.

The loud-ass news channel on his living room flat screen television distracted him from concentrating, especially when they were speaking on shit that he was trying to slow down on. Every other day it would be a shooting, and the next week, your entire block was ecstatic to see who would get their dumb ass killed for accepting that title. Who didn't want to run the hood? It was made for the people to get together and earn that cake, to make sure the elderly, women, and children received whatever necessary to build more. The vibration of Precious's laptop sounded off loudly.

Ryan walked over to the dining room table and stared at the video chat blinking repeatedly. Turning the computer towards him, he answered the chat. Precious's gorgeous face appeared, blowing him a sexy kiss.

"Hey love."

"Wassup, baby?" Ryan grinned with joy from sight of that wonderful smile.

"Nothing much. I'm leaving my third period course, and I feel like a couch potato. I don't remember getting no work done, 'cause I just couldn't stop thinking about somebody." She rolled her eyes playfully.

"You must wanna fight?" Ryan flashed her a fake mug.

Giggling, Precious pulled a tan folder from her bag. Flipping it open, she held a piece of paper up to the screen. "Do you know what this is?"

Ryan turned his head to get a better look at the paper. "I still can't see it, Precious. Move them itty bitty-ass hands out the way.

"Boy, my hands not little. Shut up." She laughed, raising her hand at the camera. "It say 'legal contract', fathead. Do you remember when I told you about the school ball events for their faculty, and new students?"

"Yeah, the little dance thing they do every month down there."

"It's a ball, smart guy." Precious squinted her eyes.

"It's all the same. Is there something important going on this month?" Ryan's phone started to vibrate inside his pocket. Pulling it out, he viewed Demerea's name and placed it face down on the table until his video with Precious ended.

"So, the professor of my college wants to throw the events in more of a classy style. The events are very beautiful, but the school's gym is just not sufficient. They want to cut you a check and host the events inside of the club, once a month. The club is big enough to hold fifteen hundred people. That's around the same limit of guests for the college ball. From what I see on this paper, I would suggest that you consider it. Not only is it a decent proposal for more publicity and ratings on the club, the money they're offering will be for a twelve event contract. It's for two hundred thousand dollars." Precious said that shit like it was only a few measly hundreds.

"Two hundred racks to throw their events in our club? Sign that motherfucker." He moved his face closer to the camera like he was about to jump through the computer screen.

Giggling at his reaction, Precious stared into the phone. "This is a big move for you right here. I'm the queen of all my classrooms, so I have plenty of supporters behind me," she boasted with her lips poked out.

"I can't believe this, man. How did you pull something like this?" He smirked at her with a curious grin.

Crossing her fingers, she blew him a kiss. "After my last course, I'm heading home. I should be there around ten." Precious reminded him.

"I guess I'll see you then." Ryan licked his lips

Waving her fingers, she snickered and ended the video chat. It was starting to become a natural feeling with being respectful, but honest around Precious. She accepted the real Ryan. It was a plus to have her support and love. The rest was going to be handled by him personally. Those were the rules of a man.

Thinking about the business with her uncle, Ryan grabbed his jacket and car keys. In order to be sure shit flowed smoothly with Lucci, he had to be ten steps ahead. Nothing would stop this deal from becoming a two-week routine. If Lucci's rich-ass customer was happy, Ryan could smile for years without breaking a sweat. Even though his confidence was rocket ship status, facts came from the footwork. You still had to show the streets why not to think twice with their loyalty. When Lucci handled the deal tomorrow, the agreement would shoot him up to the big league overnight.

Ryan couldn't help but to flash a devilish smile knowing that his reach and ties were about to rise. It was the power that people respected. That respect was only conquered through one path: fear.

Chapter 20

Demerea's house party
8:25 p.m.

The slow weekday seemed to be dragging along throughout the morning, but now the darkness was swallowing the blue skies, changing the sunny peaceful zone into a dark city of sin. It was said that the devil roamed at night when you indulged with the dirty deeds of Wilmington, Delaware. It was a city where you just didn't expect the unexpected.

Demerea's spot was flooded from the back rooms to the backyard. Ass was being popped from all angles, and the music was pumping so loud that the guests could feel it in their chests when the beat dropped. Food was prepared by the loads, and nearly every corner was lightning up a fat blunt of exotic marijuana.

Demerea decided to throw a bash after getting the news of being able to model for her club's magazine. The subscription would be published through a major line of people who signed a few big checks for the right woman. That shit was a main priority when she was first offered the deal, but still and all, she had things out of order, which forced her hands to push the limit a little harder for what she wanted.

Demerea turned around to get a drink and happened to spot Faith sectioned off in the kitchen by herself. She slid through all of her close friends and relatives in order to reach the area.

"Faith, why the hell are you over here looking all delicious by yourself, bitch?" Demerea kissed her cheek. Her friend's old classy style was being trashed and forcing something new out of her. The tight blue Valentino jeans on her body were hugging extra tight, and her breasts were sitting up pretty, thanks to the tight and sexy white Dion Lee shirt she rocked perfectly. Her makeup was banging and gave her that bad girl look all over again.

"I ain't got no reason to be around the rest of these bum-ass bitches. I can dance and talk to my damn self." Faith moved her hips with the music.

"Girl, don't nobody be mad about shit like that anymore. When you mad, replace it with dick, and you'll laugh about it tomorrow. Call your man now." Demerea laughed at the small joke.

Faith's expression tightened quickly, "Is that shit supposed to be funny?"

"Girl, calm down. It was just a joke." Demerea could see the seriousness pumping through her fire red pupils. "I was only trying to cheer you up. I don't know why you getting mad when I warned you about him. I know you, Faith. You will try and fight this bitch and cause confusion, but Ryan's ass is the problem." She shrugged, looking down at the time on her cell phone.

Faith folded her arms and closed their distance. "I wouldn't give a fuck who she supposed to be or what the hell any of her plans is. I was left for a bitch that he barely even knows, and I'm irreplaceable. My head isn't screwed on right, and that dirty-ass nigga just think he won. I am the triple cross, and you can bet that shit," she vented and took a sip of her cup.

Demerea knew exactly how shit was about to go when it came to niggas. Nothing changed but the lies, and if you at least threw that ass back in the bed, you had a chance on keeping him from not fucking your sister or mom. It was a jungle when it came to what you wanted, and some people would do whatever, maybe even more than you, to get what you wanted so badly. "I'm sorry, Faith. I didn't mean to upset you. I know that Ryan running around here with this little cute-ass suburb girl who probably got a lot of money, but that bitch ain't you. She can't do the shit that you do, or show the same love to him. I just don't want you to be stressing around here, all depressed and shit."

Faith's mind accepted the encouraging words from her friend, but at the time, it just wasn't settling in. Ryan was living it up, and that shit was surely not about to last. The pain he caused split Faith's heart in two. She tried to focus in order for her anger to stay concealed. It felt like torture, and the stanky suburb bitch Precious wasn't making it any better. "I'm not about to keep dwelling on Ryan's actions. I'll show him better. There is no such thing as leaving me when I've placed my all into this shit. Most bitches talk and can't back that shit up. That ain't me." Faith tossed the last of her liquor back and trashed the empty cup.

"I understand. You look horrible, girl. Ever since this shit crunk up, there ain't been no smiles or nothing from you."

Faith's eyes rolled over to Ryan and DJ stepping through the front door of Demerea's home. "Yeah, I think I'm gonna go home and get some rest. My head just started to hurt."

"Are you sure, girl?" Demerea looked at her with a pouty face.

"Yeah." Faith leaned in to hug her friend. Turning to leave, she was sure to step out of Ryan's path before he could pass her. Without saying a word, she quickly departed.

Demerea's eyes followed Faith until she left. It was sad how things could go when it came to relationships, but that was life. You had to go hard for what you wanted. There was no other way to have happiness.

Her vision locked in on Ryan talking to a few guests. His appearance was looking greater than ever. He rocked a beige Louis Vuitton sweater with a pair of crispy fitted Robin jeans. His feet sported a pair of clean loafers that completed his fresh entrance. He truly looked good enough to eat.

After fixing the boys up a strong drink, Demerea moved through the crowd until she reached the small group where Ryan stood running his mouth. All the thirsty little chickens tried to throw that ass extra harder since he and DJ had posted against the living room wall. That shit was about to end. "Here you go, Ryan. I'm glad you could make it." She held the cup in front of him and passed one to DJ.

Ryan grabbed the cup with a smile. He couldn't help but check out her little freaky-ass outfit. The tight Gucci one-piece jumper gripped every curve perfectly, and the look in her eyes asked him to take it off. "Wassup, girl? How the hell you fit all that in this shit?" He pointed down at her little sexy suit.

Laughing, she popped her booty a little. "It ain't much, but I be trying."

"You trying too damn hard then." DJ pulled out his phone and imitated a photographer.

"I know that's right. I should have went to school for it." She winked her eye. "Ryan, I didn't even think you were coming, to be honest. I just told DJ to pass the word."

"Facts. You know I was coming to pop my shit. I seen ya little friend leave when I came, but I don't give a damn," Ryan mentioned before taking a big swig of the tasty drink.

"Yeah, fuck all that. She mad with me too." Demerea shrugged. "I know how that's gonna go, but on another note, I need to speak with you about something."

"Is everything alright?" Ryan asked before chugging the last drop in his cup.

Demerea cut her eyes over to DJ before whispering in Ryan's ear. "It's more personal. We need to be alone."

Nodding with a smirk, he passed her back the cup. "Fix me one more, and I'll meet you in the back room."

She could tell from the smile he was ready to beat some pussy down, and that was damn sure the goal. "I'll be right there," she giggled before heading back over to the kitchen. Grabbing the juice from the back of her freezer, she fixed another cup. Nothing was about to fuck up this new shot, and Ryan was going to be the one to help her.

Glancing at the time on her phone, Demerea decided to have a couple minutes of fun until she handled the business. Dick wasn't a necessity, but on behalf of Ryan, any situation could wait for some of his good fucking. Picking up the drink, she headed to the back with a smile. The games were about to begin.

Chris Green

Chapter 21

10:35 p.m.

Precious got off the expressway and quickly stopped at the corner store to grab a few things. She knew that Ryan was a big fan of food, so she decided to give him a taste of her skills. It didn't take long to snatch up the ingredients for a great recipe. The sweet feeling of tasting her chicken Alfredo was like none other. If she could put a smile on his face from that, then his ass was gonna have to strap up the gloves.

Leaving the food market, she headed directly for Ryan's apartment. School and working were taking a toll, but the new connection with him was something that couldn't be replaced. Love didn't strike Precious as a teen for the most common reasons. It was hard to find true passion in a young man. The goal was to fall for a real one, and be sure to hold on tight. After many years of strong patience, she hoped that the statement could finally be placed to rest.

After ten minutes of riding down the hot-ass block, Precious reached Ryan's street and pulled down in front of his building. Noticing that his car still wasn't there, she decided to use the key he gave her to get inside and cook up a real woman meal.

After stepping out of her car, Precious headed for the backseat to collect the groceries. She leaned inside, grabbed the six bags, and reached for the small bottle of Tropicana that was laying on the floorboard. "Dis boy got me 'bout to break my damn back to be nice," Precious mumbled to herself. Ryan was surely lucky, and hopefully he could be good enough to express himself about building them a real relationship. That was all she wanted: love.

The sound of a pistol cocking back loudly froze her limbs completely. "Don't move, bitch!" the voice of a woman hissed low enough for only Precious to hear.

Instead of lying down inside the backseat of her car like she intended, the thought of a woman robbing her was not about to fly the easy way.

"Bitch, I said don't move," the female stressed as Precious swiftly backed out of the car to face her attacker.

Turning around, she gasped, and before her lips could utter a word, a huge bright flash erupted, stopping all movement.

BOOM!

To Be Continued...
Midnight Cartel 3
Coming Soon

Submission Guideline

Submit the first three chapters of your completed manuscript to ldpsubmissions@gmail.com, subject line: Your book's title. The manuscript must be in a .doc file and sent as an attachment. Document should be in Times New Roman, double spaced and in size 12 font. Also, provide your synopsis and full contact information. If sending multiple submissions, they must each be in a separate email.

Have a story but no way to send it electronically? You can still submit to LDP/Ca$h Presents. Send in the first three chapters, written or typed, of your completed manuscript to:

LDP: Submissions Dept
Po Box 870494
Mesquite, Tx 75187

DO NOT send original manuscript. Must be a duplicate.

Provide your synopsis and a cover letter containing your full contact information.

Thanks for considering LDP and Ca$h Presents.

Chris Green

184

KILL ZONE **II**

BAE BELONGS TO ME III

SOUL OF A MONSTER III

By **Aryanna**

THE COST OF LOYALTY **III**

By **Kweli**

CHAINED TO THE STREETS II

By **J-Blunt**

KING OF NEW YORK V

COKE KINGS IV

BORN HEARTLESS IV

By **T.J. Edwards**

GORILLAZ IN THE BAY V

De'Kari

THE STREETS ARE CALLING II

Duquie Wilson

KINGPIN KILLAZ IV

STREET KINGS III

PAID IN BLOOD III

CARTEL KILLAZ IV

Hood Rich

SINS OF A HUSTLA II

ASAD

TRIGGADALE III

Elijah R. Freeman

KINGZ OF THE GAME V

Playa Ray

Chris Green

SLAUGHTER GANG IV
RUTHLESS HEART III
By Willie Slaughter
THE HEART OF A SAVAGE II
By Jibril Williams
FUK SHYT II
By Blakk Diamond
THE DOPEMAN'S BODYGAURD II
By Tranay Adams
TRAP GOD II
By Troublesome
YAYO III
A SHOOTER'S AMBITION II
By S. Allen
GHOST MOB
Stilloan Robinson
KINGPIN DREAMS II
By Paper Boi Rari
CREAM
By Yolanda Moore
SON OF A DOPE FIEND II
By Renta
FOREVER GANGSTA II
By Adrian Dulan
LOYALTY AIN'T PROMISED
By Keith Williams
THE PRICE YOU PAY FOR LOVE II

By Destiny Skai

THE LIFE OF A HOOD STAR

By Rashia Wilson

TOE TAGZ III

By Ah'Million

CONFESSIONS OF A GANGSTA II

By Nicholas Lock

PAID IN KARMA II

By **Meesha**

I'M NOTHING WITHOUT HIS LOVE II

By Monet Dragun

CAUGHT UP IN THE LIFE II

By Robert Baptiste

NEW TO THE GAME II

By **Malik D. Rice**

Life of a Savage II

By **Romell Tukes**

Available Now

RESTRAINING ORDER **I & II**

By **CA$H & Coffee**

LOVE KNOWS NO BOUNDARIES **I II & III**

By **Coffee**

RAISED AS A GOON I, II, III & IV

BRED BY THE SLUMS I, II, III

Chris Green

BLAST FOR ME I & II

ROTTEN TO THE CORE I II III

A BRONX TALE I, II, III

DUFFEL BAG CARTEL I II III

HEARTLESS GOON I II III IV

A SAVAGE DOPEBOY I II

HEARTLESS GOON I II III

DRUG LORDS I II III

By **Ghost**

LAY IT DOWN **I & II**

LAST OF A DYING BREED

BLOOD STAINS OF A SHOTTA I & II III

By **Jamaica**

LOYAL TO THE GAME I II III

LIFE OF SIN I, II III

By **TJ & Jelissa**

BLOODY COMMAS I & II

SKI MASK CARTEL I II & III

KING OF NEW YORK I II,III IV

RISE TO POWER I II III

COKE KINGS I II III

BORN HEARTLESS I II III

By **T.J. Edwards**

IF LOVING HIM IS WRONG…I & II

LOVE ME EVEN WHEN IT HURTS I II III

By **Jelissa**

WHEN THE STREETS CLAP BACK I & II III

By **Jibril Williams**

A DISTINGUISHED THUG STOLE MY HEART I II & III

LOVE SHOULDN'T HURT I II III IV

RENEGADE BOYS I II III IV

PAID IN KARMA

By **Meesha**

A GANGSTER'S CODE I &, II III

A GANGSTER'S SYN I II III

THE SAVAGE LIFE I II III

CHAINED TO THE STREETS

By J-Blunt

PUSH IT TO THE LIMIT

By **Bre' Hayes**

BLOOD OF A BOSS **I, II, III, IV, V**

SHADOWS OF THE GAME

By **Askari**

THE STREETS BLEED MURDER **I, II & III**

THE HEART OF A GANGSTA I II& III

By **Jerry Jackson**

CUM FOR ME I II III IV V

An **LDP Erotica Collaboration**

BRIDE OF A HUSTLA **I II & II**

THE FETTI GIRLS **I, II& III**

CORRUPTED BY A GANGSTA I, II III, IV

BLINDED BY HIS LOVE

THE PRICE YOU PAY FOR LOVE

By **Destiny Skai**

Chris Green

WHEN A GOOD GIRL GOES BAD
By **Adrienne**
THE COST OF LOYALTY I II
By Kweli
A GANGSTER'S REVENGE **I II III & IV**
THE BOSS MAN'S DAUGHTERS I II III IV V
A SAVAGE LOVE **I & II**
BAE BELONGS TO ME I II
A HUSTLER'S DECEIT I, II, III
WHAT BAD BITCHES DO I, II, III
SOUL OF A MONSTER I II
KILL ZONE
By **Aryanna**
A KINGPIN'S AMBITON
A KINGPIN'S AMBITION **II**
I MURDER FOR THE DOUGH
By **Ambitious**
TRUE SAVAGE I II III IV V VI
DOPE BOY MAGIC I, II
MIDNIGHT CARTEL I II
By **Chris Green**
A DOPEBOY'S PRAYER
By **Eddie "Wolf" Lee**
THE KING CARTEL **I, II & III**
By **Frank Gresham**
THESE NIGGAS AIN'T LOYAL **I, II & III**
By **Nikki Tee**

190

Midnight Cartel 2

GANGSTA SHYT **I II &III**
By **CATO**
THE ULTIMATE BETRAYAL
By **Phoenix**
BOSS'N UP **I , II & III**
By **Royal Nicole**
I LOVE YOU TO DEATH
By Destiny J
I RIDE FOR MY HITTA
I STILL RIDE FOR MY HITTA
By **Misty Holt**
LOVE & CHASIN' PAPER
By **Qay Crockett**
TO DIE IN VAIN
SINS OF A HUSTLA
By **ASAD**
BROOKLYN HUSTLAZ
By **Boogsy Morina**
BROOKLYN ON LOCK I & II
By **Sonovia**
GANGSTA CITY
By **Teddy Duke**
A DRUG KING AND HIS DIAMOND I & II III
A DOPEMAN'S RICHES
HER MAN, MINE'S TOO I, II
CASH MONEY HO'S
By Nicole Goosby

191

Chris Green

TRAPHOUSE KING **I II & III**

KINGPIN KILLAZ I II III

STREET KINGS I II

PAID IN BLOOD **I II**

CARTEL KILLAZ I II III

By **Hood Rich**

LIPSTICK KILLAH **I, II, III**

CRIME OF PASSION I II & III

By **Mimi**

STEADY MOBBN' **I, II, III**

THE STREETS STAINED MY SOUL

By **Marcellus Allen**

WHO SHOT YA **I, II, III**

SON OF A DOPE FIEND

Renta

GORILLAZ IN THE BAY **I II III IV**

DE'KARI

TRIGGADALE I II

Elijah R. Freeman

GOD BLESS THE TRAPPERS I, II, III

THESE SCANDALOUS STREETS I, II, III

FEAR MY GANGSTA I, II, III

THESE STREETS DON'T LOVE NOBODY I, II

BURY ME A G I, II, III, IV, V

A GANGSTA'S EMPIRE I, II, III, IV

THE DOPEMAN'S BODYGAURD

Tranay Adams

192

THE STREETS ARE CALLING
Duquie Wilson
MARRIED TO A BOSS… I II III
By Destiny Skai & Chris Green
KINGZ OF THE GAME I II III IV
Playa Ray
SLAUGHTER GANG I II III
RUTHLESS HEART I II
By Willie Slaughter
THE HEART OF A SAVAGE
By Jibril Williams
FUK SHYT
By Blakk Diamond
DON'T F#CK WITH MY HEART I II
By Linnea
ADDICTED TO THE DRAMA I II III
By Jamila
YAYO I II
A SHOOTER'S AMBITION
By S. Allen
TRAP GOD
By Troublesome
FOREVER GANGSTA
By Adrian Dulan
TOE TAGZ I II
By Ah'Million
KINGPIN DREAMS

Chris Green

By Paper Boi Rari
CONFESSIONS OF A GANGSTA
By Nicholas Lock
I'M NOTHING WITHOUT HIS LOVE
By Monet Dragun
CAUGHT UP IN THE LIFE
By Robert Baptiste
NEW TO THE GAME
By **Malik D. Rice**
Life of a Savage
By **Romell Tukes**

BOOKS BY LDP'S CEO, CA$H

TRUST IN NO MAN

TRUST IN NO MAN 2

TRUST IN NO MAN 3

BONDED BY BLOOD

SHORTY GOT A THUG

THUGS CRY

THUGS CRY 2

THUGS CRY 3

TRUST NO BITCH

TRUST NO BITCH 2

TRUST NO BITCH 3

TIL MY CASKET DROPS

RESTRAINING ORDER

RESTRAINING ORDER 2

IN LOVE WITH A CONVICT

Coming Soon

BONDED BY BLOOD 2

BOW DOWN TO MY GANGSTA

Chris Green